T0385194

THE BUREAU

Also by Eoin McNamee

Resurrection Man
The Last of Deeds and Love in History
Love in History
The Blue Tango
Orchid Blue
Blue Is the Night
The Ultras
12.23
The Vogue

THE BUREAU

Eoin McNamee

riverrun

First published in Great Britain in 2025 by

riverrun

An imprint of

Quercus Editions Limited
Carmelite House
50 Victoria Embankment
London EC4Y 0DZ

An Hachette UK company

The authorised representative in the EEA is Hachette Ireland,
8 Castlecourt Centre, Dublin 15, D15 XTP3, Ireland (email: info@hbgi.ie)

A CIP catalogue record for this book is available
from the British Library.

Hardback 978 1 52944 042 3
Trade Paperback 978 1 52944 043 0
Ebook 978 1 52944 045 4

3

Typeset by CC Book Production
Printed and bound in Great Britain by Clays Ltd, Elcograf S.p.A.

Papers used by riverrun are from well-managed forests and other responsible sources.

For Shane
Made it brother

Fragment of letter from Paddy Farrell to my father, Brendan
McNamee, May 1983:

CORK PRISON CENSORED

Patrick Farrell

Cork Prison

Rathmore Road

10 NLG 1983

2 NLG 1983

*Dear Brendan how are things out there. I just thought Id
drop you a few lines as its sunday here and we have plenty of
time on our hands. Well first of all I want to thank sweeney
for coming up*

tell larry also. he can drop me a line if there's any queries regarding anything. You need not show him this letter. I wonder how they got on with that business that I had arranged with your wee man. Any word from him? Did he come to see you. What do you think of this business Brendan that I'm supposed to be involved in. I think it might be a good idea to try and get proof of where I was between those dates that were mentioned. What did you think of that barrister. I suppose he'd be good enough for the trial

I meant too have a chat with you the last

End of letter fragment.

The letter is the only evidence that these things had indeed happened and they happened in the way I describe them. Some stories seem to tell themselves and other stories wish to remain untold. It is uncertain which this is.

They were in an upstairs bedroom. Paddy was naked on the bed. Lorraine was on the floor on top of the shotgun. The room becoming its own forensics. Blood spatter. Spread pattern. The room arranging itself into false settings, looking faked up, tired, frayed at the edges. It's a girl's bedroom in a suburban house, shabby, the slippers under the wardrobe, concert tickets Blu-tacked to the wall, the loved spaces. The things a girl kept on her dressing table, yellow puckers in the varnish, someone has lit a cigarette and left it poised on the edge. You can see Paddy lying on the bed watching her do her make-up, the little inner gestures, the pursing, the dabbing with tissue. Working your way towards the inner self. That was what all the mirrored cases were about, the brushes and pencils, the clasps and trinketry.

Come quickly. Paddy is shot.

Boyle O'Reilly Terrace faces the back of the Lourdes hospital. The incinerators and morgues. Two-storey red-brick houses with small gardens to the front. A fit-up for a suburban sex crime, for back garden prowlers. There are few people walking. An elderly woman, a man with a sports bag, a lone, misdirected look in his eyes. The houses are red-brick, semi-detached. The doors PVC with diamond pane inset. These are long vistas, you can picture it after dark, the stalked-through night-time streets. The man with the sports bag looked as if he had packed for this.

At the rear of the terrace is the Lourdes stadium where track and field events were held. It had fallen into decay, grass growing through the asphalt of the running track, the handrails bent, tarnished. It had been built for those who would be ardent in the everyday, the spike marks still visible on the starting blocks, a rotted singlet on a crush barrier memorial to their strivings.

Beyond the Lourdes stadium is St Peter's graveyard and St Peter's church where the mummified head of the seventeenth-century martyr Blessed Oliver Plunkett is preserved in a catafalque. Beside the catafalque is the door of the cell where Plunkett was held in Newgate prison before being hanged, drawn and quartered. The road that runs along the back of these buildings is known as the Twenties.

Paddy is shot. Lorraine is shot.

They were found by Lorraine's stepfather Dessie Wilton. He had returned home for work with Peggy Farrell, his common-law wife and Lorraine's mother, at teatime. They saw Paddy Farrell's burgundy Mercedes 320SL parked outside. Wilton said they watched a football match on television in the living room downstairs, although the *Irish Independent* reported he had earlier looked into the darkened room when they entered the house and saw what he thought was Paddy asleep on the bed. They could hear Paddy and Lorraine's mobile phones ringing upstairs.

Wilton had looked for Lorraine's handbag after the match. He found it in the kitchen and looked inside. He did not state why he was looking for the handbag or why he looked inside. He found a letter to Lorraine's sister. There was money inside the envelope. On reading the letter he had gone upstairs and opened the bedroom door. Lorraine was in a crouched position. Not flung against the wall by the force of the blast. Crouched in interior darkness, cold and alabaster, a tomb gift set before the naked masked man. Wilton thinking they were

still alive until he saw the blood on the naked bodies, a black
PVC dress lying on the floor, in the sad light of their own
imperfections, all skin pucker and elastic mark.

Peggy heard him cry out. He told Peggy not to go into the
room then he had gone to his neighbour's, Townley, who was
an undertaker. Wilton asked Townley to come to the house.
Paddy is shot, Lorraine is shot, he said. Come quickly, Dessie
said. Tell me what you see. Who would know more about death
than an undertaker? Peggy is walking up and down outside.
Dessie is trying to hurry the undertaker. Come quickly. There's
blood everywhere.

The statements made to the police had a rehearsed feel to
them. Several days before Lorraine Farrell had gone to Townley,
the same Patrick Townley who was called by Dessie Wilton
who had seen her almost naked and dead in her bedroom. She
had paid him £200 for a double grave. The court was told that
Lorraine had borrowed a shotgun from licensed firearms dealer
Leo Murray.

Firearms dealers. Undertakers.

Lorraine would have worked out the funeral arrangements.
There would be lilies on the altar because they were death
flowers but also pure and Lorraine liked the words lily of the

valley. In certain circumstances of purity she thought that she might indeed herself be a Lily of the Valley. There was a girl from Newry who sang Panis Angelicus at weddings and funerals and Lorraine had left money for her. She had to be paid and Lorraine was a girl who paid her debts.

Lorraine crouched by the bed. This was not the renegade end she had imagined for Paddy and herself, gunned down in their defiance by lessers, sprawled on some midnight roadway. To shoot yourself with a shotgun you had to squat and put the stock of the gun between your ankles and the barrel under your chin, the barrel warm and the saltpetre reek of the discharged cartridge in your nostrils. Then you reached down and hooked your fingers around the back of the trigger guard and worked your thumb onto the trigger and then you put the barrel of the gun into your mouth.

Paddy's underwear was missing. His shirt was found in the living room. His attaché case was gone. The briefcase he carried everywhere with him. His case that allegedly contained 70,000 euros. His wallet was not found.

The *Drogheda Argus* reported that two yellow roses had been left at the gateway of the house. The neighbours were said to be in a state of shock. They said she was a lovely girl. They said that she 'always had a smile' for you. The reporter spoke to a former boyfriend who said that she loved her car, a Peugeot 307. He also said she was a lovely girl but highly strung. The reporter was told that she had been 'very active on the social scene' at one stage but had not been seen about local nightspots since she met Paddy and started spending time with him in Newry.

Come quickly.

Forensics said that wadding from two shotgun cartridges had been removed from the ceiling of Lorraine's room. This meant that four shots had been fired. The first police witness said that the room had been 'covered in shotgun pellets'. The two extra shots had to have been fired after Paddy had been killed. He would have reacted to a shot fired into the ceiling.

How loud the shotgun blasts must have sounded in the small room. A shotgun blast at close range creates 165 decibels. Pain begins at 125 decibels and 165 decibels is just below the level where hearing tissue starts to die.

It feels as if Lorraine had deliberately set out to leave an evidential trail. The fact that she bought a double grave in the week preceding the shootings. The fact that she had a shotgun on loan. The loan of the shotgun was not commented on at the inquest. There was no testimony as to whether the seller had asked Lorraine if she possessed a licence for the gun or if she left any security to ensure that she would pay for it. The seller said that he formed the impression that she was experienced at clay pigeon shooting. The shotgun was four feet long and Lorraine was five-foot-two. Did she handle it expertly, break it open, peer down the barrel to make sure it was clear of residue and that there was no corrosion or pitting? A bag of 70mm cartridges was also found in her bedroom. The gun dealer said that he had not given her any cartridges.

Lorraine is shot.

The *Sunday World* published two photographs of Lorraine Farrell. It is surprising that more do not exist. Before she took up with Paddy Lorraine was popular and well known. You'd get nightclub shots in the local paper, charity fashion shows, sports days. In the photograph used by the *Sunday World*, a head shot, she looks as if she's walking and has glanced up just as the photograph was taken from the front and side. It is a thin-lipped look, the eyes narrowed, distrustful of the camera. Her face is pinched. Her hair is blonde, parted in the centre which makes her face longer and thinner, the effect accentuated by the blow-dry which leaves a fringe hanging over her eyes. She's shifty, a moll, some brazen outside a courtroom. You know it's not going to end well.

The other photograph shows the Lorraine that the neighbours talked about, the popular, friendly girl. It looks as if she is doing promotion work. Facing the camera, her smile is all teeth, there was always a bit of dazzle to her. She's wearing a sleeveless vest top, her hair in blonde highlights, she's the kind of girl that newspapers call vivacious.

In most murder-suicides the perpetrator will be male. He will kill his wife or partner and then he will kill himself. He may or may not kill the children. There are examples of murder-suicide where the perpetrator is female but these are rare. These killings happen most frequently among the older age group and those who have been in long-term relationships often characterized by abuse directed by the male partner towards the female partner.

Women who kill husbands or intimate partners whether or not they subsequently take their own lives will plan the killing meticulously. When firearms are available the weapon is bought or borrowed then concealed until the opportunity to use it arises. Loose ends are tidied up. Letters are written. Provision is made for children. In most instances the victim will have been abusive. In most instances the woman will express relief that her ordeal has come to an end.

In cases of murder-suicide committed by a woman there is invariably a passage of time between the killing of the spouse and the suicide. There will be a wandering off, the suicide's body found at some distance from the dead spouse. In a garden or a summer house, somewhere outdoors. Not to cause a mess. Not to cause any more mess than you already have. There are two distinct acts. You turn the gun on your partner then after some time you turn it on yourself. You take your killing self to one side and live with it for a while. There is room for regret, not regret that you have killed, but that you are in the garden and that it is the evening, the last evening. You take your killing self to one side and live with it for a while and then you end it.

Lorraine borrowed a shotgun. She bought a grave for two persons although she must have known that Paddy would never be buried with her. She made arrangements for her own funeral. The undertaker Townley said that when she bought a grave from him she enquired about funeral arrangements in general. She also enquired about embalming. That part fits. But there seem to be no recorded instances of a young woman carrying out a murder-suicide in the manner of the death of Paddy Farrell and and the suicide of Lorraine Farrell. The patterns of behaviour break down. Paddy was not abusive. His death did not come at the end of years of bullying. He was not sprawled snoring on an armchair. She was not some frayed end-of-her-tether wife, harried into the jaws of death. They were lovers in the act of love. There did not seem to be two distinct acts, although no opinion was expressed at the inquest as to the time lapse between Paddy's death and Lorraine's death. But there is no indication that she left the room, that she walked the house, her skin spotted with Paddy's blood, with skull fragments all speckled about her. She stayed there until she finished the job.

The couple had been dead for hours when Peggy and Dessie

called. The sound of the football match downstairs, the crowd roar, the swelling chant carrying upstairs, the massed humanity. The phones ringing upstairs all through the match. There's something about the unanswered calls, the dead naked couple summoned. As if they could be called back from their shared dark, the phones beeping in the unlit room, the messaged stillness.

Paddy is shot. Lorraine is shot.

One

The Imperial Hotel, Dundalk. Racing on the television above the bar. Border nights. Renegade nights. The windows in smoked glass. After dark you felt the town gone rogue, men in black suits and white shirts coming in from the outlands, paying in cash. Above the Old Spice and bootleg Chanel the place reeked of the illicit, border runs in the dusk light.

Brendan was sitting at the counter watching the news. Lorraine came up to get a drink. Brendan the only one who looked at what was happening in the world outside. Brendan wearing an Aquascutum coat gone grubby at the pockets and the lapels. She'd heard about him. A struck-off lawyer from Newry. There'd been some kind of scandal, shady dealings. The locals went to him for advice. When something's gone wrong, when someone was looking for you he was the person to go to and there was always someone looking for you in these frontier years. He knew the rogue lawyers, the on-the-take customs agents. He drank with the alcoholic judges and the nerve-shot policemen. Being caught was where the game started. Lorraine went to buy a drink and put her elbows on the bar and he smiled at her, the teeth stained with tobacco, a grimness to the smile, drawing it up from some haggard place within. A Bacardi, she said, rum and Coke. You waited for the come-back, men came out with it every time you ordered a Bacardi, *a leg-opener*, but Brendan didn't say anything. He crooked his finger at the barman, ordered her drink and his.

'Can I take a cigarette?' He turned the pack towards her.

'You shouldn't be smoking,' he said, 'you should give them up.'

'I only take one when I have a drink.'

'Doesn't matter. Tell you what. Stop here and now. I'll give you twenty pounds for every day you stay off them.' This was something that Brendan did, he'd try to bribe you away from yourself, everything priced, there was always some unloved part of yourself to be cashed in.

'Can a girl not go powder her nose without someone chatting up her man?' Jean stepped between Lorraine and Brendan. Girl was pushing it, she'd be what Lorraine's mother called mutton dressed as lamb. Her skirts were too short for the skinny legs on her. Everything had a gilded clasp, everything had a knock-off look, border market fake imports, her handbags and collars and the amount of make-up slapped on.

'I hope the child wasn't annoying you, sweetheart, while your Jean wasn't here to keep an eye on you.'

When Jean talked to Brendan she had this little girl voice. Lorraine could hear the undertones and there was nothing little girl to it whatsoever, but men are like that. They liked the girlish voices. They liked a pleading tone.

'I was only getting a drink and he spoke to me,' Lorraine said. 'Take it handy and excuse me please I'm going to the bathroom.'

Jean followed Lorraine into the toilets. Both of them knowing what was at stake for the women you'd meet after midnight in the Imperial toilets, the provincial girls, Saturday night bringing out what had failed them during the week, lipstick-stained tissues in the waste basket, tear-stained tissues. The night's hurts brought here, the heartbroken and the wan. A pale, drunk girl was crying in the corner. The crying seemed to generate light about her, two friends talking to her softly, she was stranded on some ledge of herself and the fall would be long.

Jean was waiting for Lorraine when she came out of a cubicle.

'You keep your fucking hands off him, your hands and your fucking eyes off him or I'll scrab them out for you.'

'What do you think I am?'

'I know what you fucking are. You're the kind of girl men look at and see a fanny with legs, they'll use you up and throw you away like one of them there tissues.'

Jean doing the lipstick while she was talking, some cheap shade, some hellmouth red, Lorraine thought, a ring on a chipped bar glass, something like a glance, tawdry and lingering. Jean's handbag open on the surround of the sink, Lorraine could see where foundation had spilled in the handbag, a half-eaten packet of pastilles, a Kotex in its wrapper. Steradent. It was like Jean not to care who saw what was in her handbag but Lorraine was different. Anybody could open Lorraine's handbag and all they would see would be order, she liked handbags with lots of interior pockets for tweezers and emery boards, things that slotted into place. You didn't let others see the inner parts of your life and you didn't let them see the inner part of yourself.

'I'm sorry,' Lorraine said, 'I was only talking to some man at the bar.'

'Brendan's a generous man. There's them that take advantage. I hope you're not one of them.'

'I hope not.'

'You're younger than you looked in the bar. You could have an old soul. I'm a Pisces. My soul is ancient.'

Fuck you and your ancient soul Lorraine thought but she didn't say it.

Lorraine followed Jean out into the lounge. She couldn't see where her friends had gone so she sat at the bar beside Jean. Jean didn't seem to mind. She slid the drink that Brendan had bought Lorraine up the bar to her.

Brendan was talking to Jean but Lorraine could see that she wasn't listening.

Lorraine told Brendan that she had seen a kestrel hovering over the Lourdes sports grounds although she hadn't. It just felt like the kind of thing that a man like Brendan might want to hear. Brendan said that birds of prey didn't see what everyone else saw, that they had infra-red vision so that they could find little creatures hiding in the grass. No matter how much people tried to hide from them they could pick you out and you didn't even know.

'Here we go,' Jean said. 'Sheriff just walked into the saloon. Paddy Farrell. If you want a gander at him use the mirror. There's men who know they're being stared at and don't like it.'

Lorraine looked in the mirror. She would say afterwards that she was smitten straight off and had to turn her head slightly away so that Jean wouldn't see that her face had turned red. Paddy was wearing a tweed sports jacket and blue jeans. He wore a gold ring with a sovereign inset on his right hand. Short, well-built. Blue eyes. You felt the energy, deep-set and kinetic. You could tell that he was occupying the room in a different way. You wouldn't say walk, you wouldn't say strut. He found the spaces that fitted him.

'Is he coming over here?' Lorraine said.

'Damn right he is. He needs to talk to Brendan. He's been charged with assault and resisting arrest and has to make a statement. It took seven peelers to put him on the ground,' Jean said.

'Move over girls,' Paddy said. Lorraine shifted down the bar and Paddy sat beside Brendan. He smelt of Imperial Leather and Brut aftershave. He had a deep cut over his right eye. It drew attention to him, and Lorraine, who always said she had good instincts, knew that he didn't like that kind of attention. He carried a brown attaché case, he wanted to be thought of as a businessman. He wanted people to see him as on the level. Lorraine was intuitive about people, what they guarded, what they threw away thoughtlessly.

Paddy's eyebrow was puffy and swollen and it was turning yellow at the edges. He kept raising his hand to it, touching it lightly.

'What am I going to do about this, Brendan?'

'It's not going to look good in court,' Jean said. 'Looks like you've been in a fight.'

'I fucking was in a fight,' Paddy said.

'Here,' Brendan said. He took a flesh-coloured eyepatch from his pocket. 'Try that.' Paddy put the patch on. There had been a sad boy at Lorraine's school who wore an eye-patch to correct a lazy eye but the other children saw it as a

punishment and laughed at him although Lorraine was proud
of herself that she had never laughed. Paddy reminded Lorraine of the boy.

'Brilliant,' Jean said. 'You just look like you just got a sore
eye. Judge'll feel sorry for you.'

Brendan had these street lawyer tricks. Like how to pretend
that you had a breakdown when you were due in court, get
yourself admitted to a psychiatric hospital. Like you wore a suit
and tie going into an assize if you were a man. Like if you were
a woman you dressed like a widow, you filled a courtroom with
your actual sorrow.

'Can you really get yourself into the mental hospital?' Lorraine said.

'A last resort,' Brendan said, 'but yes.' Lorraine didn't think
he meant it but he did.

'The law can't touch you there,' Jean said.

When Brendan asked Lorraine if she knew how to rig a jury
she thought he was joking.

'Why would I want to know something like that?'

'Might keep you out of the prison some day,' Jean said.

'It'd be the like of you'd end up behind bars,' Lorraine said.
'None of mine ended up in trouble with the law.'

'Too cute to be caught is what you mean,' Jean said, 'too fly
by half.' But she laughed to show she didn't mean it.

*

Lorraine wanted to reach out and touch the eye, the wound, the ugly, lipped thing. In the bar shadows Paddy looked hooded by it. As if it was the future come to claim him. She wanted to reach out and touch him and tell him that everything would be alright and for him to say the same thing to her and tell her that these lone, premonitory feelings that came over her since she was small could be taken away. He looked up and smiled. She had expected his look to be dour, burdened with dishonesty, but it wasn't like that, it was a look that said what are we doing here with these people and their faithless hearts and she felt appraised and put right.

'I think I met my soulmate,' she said to Jean though without giving any thought as to what the soul is.

'He has a brave few years on you,' Jean said.

'So what?' She didn't care. She had enough of the local boys and their cars and how they liked to have you pinned, pushing you into the angle between frame and seat, working your dress above your waist, bracing against the window, the seat back, limbs grasped. Duress coming into it, your tights around your thighs, looking up at the interior light and the meshed whiteness of your knees through the nylon, the thirty denier imprint. They left you handled, sore, standing outside in the rain. There would be laddered tights, nail varnish chipped against interior surfaces, you're always marked, the imprint of plastic seat covers on your skin, underwear balled in your handbag. You could see yourself as a teenage pregnancy. Paddy wasn't like that.

Paddy was talking something to Brendan about traveller's cheques that were due to come on the market but Lorraine was only half listening and she hadn't got used to these conversations, the thief talk where everything was half said, sentences bitten off almost before they got out of your mouth.

Paddy went out to Reception and paid for a room with cash. Lorraine said what kind of an hotel is this but she already knew. Paddy walked ahead of her and didn't look back. When they got to the room he opened the door and closed it behind her. He turned the light off and she took off her clothes and lay down on the carpet. There was a lewdness to it, sprawled in the dark. He brought out abandonment in her, gutturals she had never uttered before. When he was on top of her she reached out and touched the cut above his eye. She pressed her fingers into it until she could feel the ridge of bone underneath. He didn't say a word. He kept moving, and she kept pressing into the wound and she could see his one unhurt eye fixed on her, this man on her, a look she'd never seen on a man's face before, gashed and unholy.

Two

The Bureau de Change was a rented shopfront on Water Street in Newry belonging to Brendan. There was a gangland feel to it. The front of it was fake wood with a teller's window in the middle. The window was bulletproof glass set into a heavy steel frame, the perspex abraded and hard to see through. The dual carriageway in front carried the majority of cross-border traffic going from Belfast into the border hinterlands and beyond to Dublin. The other buildings on the street were what remained of the old town when the road had been pushed through and flats built on the cleared ground. There was a shoe shop, a paint and wallpaper shop, a barber's. The owner's world had long passed, they were émigrés from some place within, far countries of the watchful heart, they'd sit at their doorways, rheumed and frail. The only ground they stood on was that of their own imagining and the Bureau took its own place among them. A yellow sign said Money Changed. There was no statement of ownership or any other welcome. From the start this was about one thing, it was about money, the getting of it, the love of it, the spending of it. If money had a religion, then this place would be its church, its grimy roadside chapel, godless.

It was all cash. You counted out the notes into hundreds, folded them over and banded them into five hundreds. Canvas bags full of used notes on the back seat. The banks demanded invoices for the goods you were buying so you faked the invoices.

'We provide a service,' Brendan said, 'people need to change money crossing the border. We change it for them and charge a percentage. Simple.' But there was nothing simple about it.

'Wherever there's money there's trouble,' Hutchie said. Hutchie had just been released from Crumlin Road prison. He had served three years of a seven-year sentence for forgery of commercial lorry driving licences. He had a beaten look, wearing an anorak and a tweed cap which he pulled down over his face. Lorraine thought he was concealing his right eye which he had lost in a car accident ten years previous and replaced with a glass eye. But Jean said he wasn't that shy about it. He would sometimes take his glass eye out in the pub and place it in a lady's drink, the lewd thing staring up at them.

'Watch him,' Jean said. 'He may only have the one eye but it's wide open all the time and it's looking out for Hutchie.'

Lorraine didn't know what made you a lady in Jean's eyes. Brendan's wife Elizabeth who lived in a big new house in Ravensdale was a lady, even though when Brendan went bankrupt he hadn't left her with a pot to piss in, Hutchie said. Nora was definitely a lady. She had worked in Brendan's lawyer office and stayed with him when he was struck off. She took no part in any activity that Hutchie referred to as bogey, a prison slang term meaning bogus or crooked, but nor was she innocent to it. Brendan said that she came from a well-off family and had been a debutante and had come out at the Connaught Hotel and had spent a year in Paris. Lorraine wondered if this readied her for the aristocracy of ruin she found herself among in the Bureau. People deferred to Nora and tried not to use swear words in her presence. She was straight-backed and wore fitted tweed suits with silk blouses. She brought an air of run-down big houses to the place, long-forgotten country balls. Regular customers who came in to change the cash they made from diesel laundering or bootleg vodka or illicit cigarettes gathered around her and she allowed them to flirt, a band of ragged gallants.

Nora always brought flowers from her garden to put on the counter in the public area. When she brought in a vase of pink flowers Bann asked her what they were called and Nora said they were called autumn crocus but when Bann turned away she whispered to Lorraine and Jean that the flowers were known as naked ladies because they had no leaves. Nora was kind to

Lorraine always. She recognizes class when she sees it, Lorraine said. Jean thought that there was pain in Nora's eyes when she looked at Lorraine, watching a good thing going bad. It was different with Jean. Nora knew what Jean was. These men and these corrupted times were what she was made for and if there was no good end then that was for her and her alone. Lorraine wasn't like that. She stayed pretty on the outside. Lorraine was always pretty no matter about that lying photograph of her in the papers but Nora looked at her as though she saw something dark and flickering and crabbed on the inside. Jean did not think it was death but it was.

Bann was the oldest. He was not in good health, he suffered from pleurisy and cirrhosis, his breathing and colour bad, he'd cough up phlegm for half the morning, his eyes always bloodshot from Captain Morgan's and was only good for errands but he'd work for drink money. Lorraine said he had a good soul. Jean said Bann was the only honest man to set foot in the Bureau and Hutchie said he didn't have the brains to be anything else. Nora said nothing but she would make him tea when he came in and got Hutchie to bring in an old bar stool where he could sit close to the heater. Nora knew these men who had chosen the forsaken over the godly and knew that if they were not to be indulged neither were they to be pitied. Bann would do the market pickups in the morning in time to have him at the bar in McCrink's at 10 a.m. where sometimes he would be joined by Brendan for a doctored coffee, black with a shot of Rémy Martin for Brendan and Captain Morgan's for Bann. It was the time of day when both men could feel expansive, the day still young enough for unexpected openings to arise, gambits to unfold, sun streaming through the narrow cobwebbed window above the door, silent men feeling a return of as much clarity as was left to them in these moments. It wasn't devotion as it might have been held in Bann's evangelical upbringing, but it was a ministry of sorts.

Paddy was on remand for assaulting policemen at a checkpoint although he said it was seven to one so who the fuck was assaulting who? He had to make a statement at Newry barracks and he brought Lorraine with him when he came to consult with Brendan. Brendan took them into a back office. There was nothing else in the office except a black safe with a brass plate on the front. He asked Lorraine what her handwriting was like which was a strange question but she answered anyway.

'My handwriting is excellent,' she said. 'I won prizes for handwriting in school.' She felt stupid that she mentioned the prize but Brendan nodded gravely.

'Good,' he said, and she liked him for it because he seemed to understand these things and how they fixed you in the world. He handed her a yellow legal pad and a pen and told her to write everything down. He lit a Silk Cut, then he dictated the statement that he wanted Paddy to give to the police. Paddy had told her that the policemen had stopped him at a checkpoint and told Paddy to get out of the car and Paddy had hit one of them but Brendan made it sound like a misunderstanding of jammed car doors and misspoken words and a trammelled man lashing out. Brendan was hard and cold and clear, and Lorraine began to understand how people talked about him as a brilliant man.

'When you give your statement just read that out, let the officer copy it and then sign it,' Brendan said.

'Is that the way it happened?' Lorraine said.

'It is now,' Brendan said.

'It can't be both,' Lorraine said, feeling the truth slipping away from her, no longer the hard and fast thing she thought it was.

'What'll I get?' Paddy asked.

'Suspended sentence,' Brendan said. 'Eighteen months or so.'

'How do you know that?' Lorraine asked.

'Because Brendan knows the fucking judge is how and he's going to give us a hand with American Express,' Hutchie said, and they all looked at him.

'Shut the fuck up, Hutchie,' Paddy said.

That was the first time Lorraine heard American Express mentioned. She didn't even know how credit cards and traveller's cheques worked but it felt glamorous. When she first bought the Peugeot 207 she'd drive to Dublin Airport and park outside the perimeter fence beside the runway, and watch the planes take off, silver-fuselaged, deep-purposed. Later Lorraine walked past the Thomas Cook travel agent's on her way to school and saw the brochures for foreign holidays.

She told Paddy that she had applied to be an air hostess, that she liked the way they walked, aloof as though they carried something of exotic destinations with them. She wanted that glam look, sent heavenward, up there in the icy spaces. When she told Paddy she had applied, he looked at her and looked away. He knew she was lying but he understood when a lie mattered and when it didn't. If the lie was about something good-hearted and aspired-to then he'd let it run. Lorraine liked when Paddy looked out for her, she liked the attention of faithless men, but in the end they both knew that the only glamour you got around here was on-the-run glamour and if you were spending time with Paddy and Brendan then you were in the market for it. It wasn't that Brendan was a bad man but he liked to concern himself with badness, badness in people and badness in things, and if you fly with the crows you get shot.

Three

Lorraine waited outside the police station until Paddy had made his statement, and then she took him to Giles Quay. Her family went there on their holidays. When people asked they liked to say they had a caravan but what they had was a railway carriage from the old GNR line left behind when the rail company went bankrupt and the track had been pulled up. The paint peeled on the weatherbeaten planks and tar melt from the asphalt roof ran down the plank sides of the carriage, and Lorraine lay awake listening to the sand hiss in the bogies, something carried up to her of ghost travellers, of old railway lines, of the unending miles.

'How the fuck did they get it here?' Paddy said.

'I don't know. They pulled it with a tractor or something.'

You had to leave your car at the car park at the beach and

walk to the caravan. Paddy brought his attaché case with him. He was wearing a check sports jacket and brown brogues. He kept looking around him as he crossed the shore, he mistrusted this place of shifting dunes and seagrasses and wildfowl in the shallows. Lorraine had planned the weekend so that there would be earnest sex, each of them left in a place of their own deserving and then afterwards there would be beach walks at dusk and fires of driftwood. 'What driftwood?' Paddy said. There were only tyre fenders and tarred rope ends from the docks at Greenore.

She thought there would be shared intimacies, the eased-into moments, not the beach covered in October sea-wreckage, cloud and rain squalls driven up the lough by the cold east wind.

'Are there any other people here?' he said.

'I don't know. Probably not. People don't come here in the winter.' She went outside to get some water from the tap. She knew that he would want to pace the interior of the carriage, check it out for ways of escaping, for hiding places. It made her uncomfortable to watch him. She didn't like to think that familiar rooms had a secret life unknown to her, that there might be places of concealment, evidence of historic crimes carried out, old stories about bloodstains that would not come out no matter how much you scrubbed and scrubbed.

She hooked the handle of the pail over the brass tap and waited for it to fill, wind off the lough shaking the marram grass on the dunes. This was the first place she had been kissed, there had been boys from the town, their names lost in the grassheads and sea winds. She'd run around with girls who travelled there for the summer holidays, coming from the northern industrial interior, Lurgan, Portadown, something hoarse and broken and insistent in their accents as if you had to be heard above yourself. Something heartbroken in them coming from and then returning to war as though they had reached this place solely to lay down their lost girlhoods. They had words for things she had never heard of. They shared Embassy Regals with her and smoked hash behind the shower block on the beach and brought tins of Evo-Stik behind the toilet blocks, coating the interior of paper bags with the glue and sniffing it, and Lorraine wondered how you could treat yourself in such a manner.

The train they called the Enterprise ran from Belfast to Dublin along the east coast. When Lorraine was small she would stand underneath the high viaduct which spanned Drogheda and see the lights of the Enterprise as though it ran alone in its own legend. You could see it from Lorraine's bedroom window, running along the skyline above the town. At night you could see the lit windows, feel the heavy diesel bogies cross the skyline and disappear from view into the deep cuttings that took it into the borderlands.

She carried the water into the carriage. Paddy was lying on his back on top of the bed. He had found a canvas railwayman's cap with a black cellulloid peak which had belonged to her father. His eyes glittered under the peak. He was naked and erect. This was not kissing in the dunes. This was not innocence.

'I'm the railway man,' he said. 'All aboard.' When she didn't move he said it low. '*All aboard.*' This time bad things whispered. This time she went towards him. She liked to get on top of Paddy. Protocols of desire to be observed, fingers guided, glancing touches. Sometimes she'd turn away from him and huddle at the edge of the bed, pretending to be hurt, that he'd left her lonely, and she'd murmur into the blankets, these tear-stained moments. And sometimes he did leave her in solitude. Exposed to her own need, the lonely winds of it.

She woke in the night to the Haulbowline lighthouse foghorn. The window was rimed with frost and when she looked out through it she could see the cold sea fog rising from the shoreline so that you could only just make out the roofs of the carriages and caravans below. She wondered if the city girls had ever really left the place. She remembered that the glue sniffing left them helpless, barely able to walk, their pale limbs afloat on their own imagining, blown aloft by dreamed winds.

After Giles Quay, Paddy said that Lorraine could have the week nights and his wife would have the weekends. That was five days to two. Lorraine would rather that he had said nothing, it made her feel bargained-over and cheap. She wanted to say that a love such as hers was not to be counted out in such a manner. Did you work that out on your calculator she wanted to say to him.

Paddy had business at the bank in Trevor Hill with Eamon McMahon. Eamon was in the oil business, Paddy said, diesel oil. He was a big man and he smiled at Lorraine when he saw her take Paddy's arm. Paddy pointed out Brendan's son in the queue. Paddy said he was a law student. He was tall and thin, something gnawed-at in him, something inside that wouldn't let him alone. The way he stood in the bank queue she wanted to tell him not to look so sneaky, with a big Adam's apple on him. He looked like security footage of someone about to try a crime, a desperate act that won't come off. He saw her looking at him. He thought about it for a bit and then he smiled at her. She wanted to smile back but how would that be right? She gave him the snoot, head in the air you think you can look at me, then Eamon leaned across and unfolded the piece of paper in his hand, showing it to both of them.

'You never seen anything like that in your life before,' he said. It was a banker's draft for a million pounds sterling.

Eamon had a partner Mackin in the oil business but you never saw him.

'He's the brains and I'm the muscle,' Eamon said.

'Eamon's right,' Hutchie said afterwards. 'There's no shortage of brain there. He'll be a rich man if he doesn't get himself killed. Or if Mackin doesn't get him killed.'

'What do you mean by that?'

'Mackin's a bit of a lover boy by all accounts. Moved in where he's not wanted.'

Jean pressed him to tell more but he wouldn't. Lorraine thought it was one of those border rumours you heard. But that didn't matter. Men along the border were as likely to act on an untruth as on a truth, sometimes more likely. She might have thought different if she had known the woman that Mackin was alleged to have moved in on, but it was always summertime at the start and you paid no heed to such things. Paddy and her always seemed to be crossing the border in fast cars, taking concession roads and unapproved roads to avoid police and army checkpoints. There would be stars and dog roses in the hedgerows and they would be the only people on the roads, outlaw nights, and Paddy would always have something good on the tape deck, country songs mostly, Lorraine liking the sad ones. She'd lean across the central console so that her head was on his chest and she was looking between the spokes of the steering wheel at the night going past. She could feel his legs flexing on the pedals and there was a smell of Old Spice. When she looked up she could see his face and wondered where his thoughts were. She could feel the vibration of the music and it felt always to be night and stars and this heartworn balladry of lovers on the run, sometimes he would take his hand from the wheel and rest it on her head. She could see his hands in the dashboard lights. He's wearing a gold Rolex with a link strap he bought in Jonesborough market. Everything's bootlegged, under the counter, sold out from under you. Did nobody say who he was? Did nobody tell her? Could she not see that there was death about him? Could he not see that there was death about her?

Four

Friday, 6th November, Churchtown, Dublin.

It's a weekday evening in the suburbs. The houses are well-kept. There are sweeping crescents, avenues lined with trees which have lost their leaves although winter hasn't bitten yet. Three men pull up in a Ford Granada and put on black balaclavas. Further down the avenue they see a teenage boy back a girl against a wall and despite the work the men are engaged in, the night work with no good end in sight, even considering what they have come for, they wish the lovers well, lost in their kiss, the mild abandon of it with winter coming and the shadows growing long, they're in no hurry and they wait in the car until the boy takes the girl by the hand and they walk off into the November evening.

The men go to the boot of the car and take out weapons.

A sawn-off shotgun, a 9mm Browning and an Armalite assault rifle. Two of the men go to the front door and the third goes around the back in case someone makes a break for it, they know what they're doing, light-footed, slipping through the shadows, assault rifles across their chests in the carry position.

The tiger kidnapping and robbery of American Express was alleged to have been carried out by Dominic McGlinchey, a paramilitary leader from Derry but who based himself in and around the border. Newspapers referred to him as Mad Dog McGlinchey but those who met him found him courteous, intelligent, thoughtful. When he was on the run he was interviewed by journalist Vincent Browne. The interview was carried out in the Rosnaree Hotel in Drogheda. The hotel was designed to resemble an American motel, long and low with car parking spaces painted at a slant to the bedroom block. But trade was sparse, the paint on the fascia boards was flaking and there was no sign of the glamour it had attempted to impart to this part of Drogheda, the dreamed-of America with the myth of road, the thrumming freeways, midnight tyre hiss, the myths of the unlocated.

Dominic McGlinchey had killed an estimated thirty-two people up until then. Dominic told Browne that when he was killing he liked to get up close to make certain. He said that he had not had enough formal firearms training to be sure of the kill from a distance. Browne said that he thought Dominic was tired, his sentences trailing off, his eyes kept finding something in the distance.

The taking over of the house comes easily to the men. They have come from the shadows and they will be obeyed. They're after the manager of the American Express branch in Grafton Street. The man looks like he might try something, there's an urge to defend, not to be seen as helpless in front of your wife. Dominic sees someone who would cry when he fought in school, he would be all fists and hot tears. Dominic looking at the wife. She can only see his eyes because of the balaclava but there is an intimacy in the look, something complicit *if all these people weren't here*. She puts her hand on her husband's arm. 'Don't try anything, they've got guns.' There's a flutter in her voice, a little fluting tone which she didn't mean to be there, and she wonders if her husband has heard it. Dominic nods at her.

'Sit down, John,' she says, and her husband sits down on an armchair.

'Are you going to kill us?' John says. The wife doesn't even look at him. If they were going to kill them they would be dead already. The men have brought that much into the room with them, an aura of assassinations, backroad slayings, sudden violent death. There's a metallic tang of blood hanging in the air, of pistol whippings. Dominic goes over to the manager and starts to talk to him. The man looks as if he has seen this moment coming his whole life, the long millennial hang of it, all of his doings confirmed intangible, his life in the shadows now when he thought it had been something honed and befitting to him, written in long elegant golf drives, the golden hair of other men's wives.

Every time one of the raiders smoked a cigarette he threw it on the floor, ground it out with his foot and then picked up the butt and put it in his pocket. The wife had offered the quiet one an ashtray with a nervous smile on her face, the gesture a mockery of her own suburban values, of the insistence that standards be maintained. Without looking at her he knocked it out of her hand. There were no grounds for these kinds of complicity, these wry encounters. These were not courtly times.

The three men remained in the house until 8 a.m. Dominic left at 8.05 with John. John unlocked the Grafton Street branch. Cash and traveller's cheques of an unknown value were removed from the safe. The cash and cheques were taken to a waiting car. When the robbery was completed the gang tore out the telephone wires in John's house before leaving. They warned the family not to contact anyone for an hour. John was left in a layby in an isolated area where he was later found.

When they left the wife went outside. It had rained and there was a dry patch where their car had been. She wanted to cry but she knew that someone would come out of the house and try to put an arm around her and how could she explain how comfortless were the years stretched out in front of her?

A police spokesman condemned the raid. He said that 'an entire family had been left in terror'. He said the men had told the family not to contact the police within four hours of them leaving the house. Chief Inspector Jack Maguire said that some of the men spoke with Northern accents and that he could not rule out paramilitary involvement in the crime. He said that the men 'had sunk to new lows' and that 'innocent lives had been put at risk'. A spokesman for American Express said that the stolen traveller's cheques were unsigned and therefore could not be cashed.

But they could be cashed. If you were clever they could be cashed.

Five

The Lorne Hotel, Clanbrassil Street, Dundalk. Lunchtime, the racing on the television, Kempton Park, Haydock, autumn race meetings, all flags and silks. Brendan's a gambler although no one really realizes how bad he's got the habit. He wins big and loses big. The bar's all brown leather seats and chrome fittings. They like the racing crowd in the Lorne, cash-rich and out to impress. But Brendan's not there to gamble this time, not on horses anyway.

'McGlinchey done the thing we talked about, American Express in Dublin,' Paddy says. Anyone looking on wouldn't know what they were talking about, most of what Paddy had to say conveyed in a hood's repertoire of deadpan looks and flat stares. The bar is busy but the seats on either side of them are empty, people just not comfortable sitting there though they don't know why.

'I heard about it.'

'Some cash got took, and a rake of traveller's cheques. Unsigned.'

'They're no good unsigned.'

'No, you can always sign them.'

'Won't work without a valid passport number. You'd need a counterfeit passport. Sign them and countersign them.'

'I haven't got a counterfeit passport.'

'No go then.'

'I've got better. I can get a hold of real ones.'

'The cheques are as good as cash then.'

'As good as. How many cheques were taken?'

'Seven hundred thousand pounds' worth.'

'Then someone's going to get a sore signing hand.'

'The bank'll probably refuse to honour them.'

'Then we'll have to make them honour them.'

'If there was a straight way to do something and a crooked way,' Jean said, 'them two men of ours would do it the crooked way. Every time.' Lorraine sat at the end of the Lorne bar close to the slot machine so that Jean could play. Lorraine thought that slot machines were vulgar but Jean didn't care.

Lorraine didn't like Paddy and Brendan being talked about in the same breath like that. She didn't think that her love with Paddy was anything like the way Jean was with Brendan.

Brendan was a chain-smoking older man with a weary heart and burdened shoulders. Jean was taking advantage of his sadness. As well, Jean made crude jokes about things that should always remain private between a man and a woman. Paddy was different. There was a wildness in Paddy, he didn't sit around counting his sins. There would be time enough for that.

'Do you think you could live without Brendan?'

Jean looked at her. 'Are you serious? I could live without any man. Half the time I don't know why women keep them around.' Those tight lines around her mouth of bitter history.

'That's the difference between you and me. I couldn't live without Paddy.'

Three weeks after the Grafton Street robbery the deal was done and Paddy went to get the traveller's cheques from Dominic. He took Lorraine with him. They drove deeper into border country than she had ever been. Past burned-out border posts, lone petrol stations at crossroads, something sentinel in their canopy lights as dusk fell. They were in a place far off and unpatrolled, beyond law and soldiery. It was winter, All Souls' Night.

At times like these Paddy was all business. Lorraine had an expression *shop face* which meant that whatever you felt or whatever row you had, you put on a smile for the customer but when Paddy was doing business there was nothing fake about it. The face he put on went all the way down to some hard, untouched place.

Dominic was staying in a semi-derelict two-storey farmhouse with the downstairs windows sealed by cement blocks. It was like a house from a film Lorraine said afterwards. Inside there was no electricity but there were Tilley lights in the downstairs rooms. There was a shotgun on the kitchen table and a revolver on a low table in the living room. The Tilley lights hissed and flickered and there was a smell of warm paraffin. Paddy moved in and out of the shadows but Dominic sat like a man graven into legend stroking his border raider's moustache.

There was movement upstairs and Paddy looked towards the ceiling.

'It's just Mary,' Dominic said. 'She said she wanted a sleep after.' Lorraine didn't need to ask what after meant. Dominic had a sated look about him though she was to learn that he was as much sated by blood as he was by sex.

The landing boards above them creaked and there were footsteps on the wooden stairs. Lorraine had never seen Mary before and never saw her again after that night. Mary had the kind of face you heard called handsome in a woman, mannish in the dim light. Here was a woman who would measure you for a grave so that her husband would put you in it. Lorraine always felt secure with Paddy but she knew that Dominic and Mary would not grant you safety in this world nor in the next.

'Pretty,' Mary said. 'What's your name?'

'Lorraine.'

'Where do you come from?'

'Drogheda.'

'And how did a Drogheda girl find herself caught up in all of this?' Lorraine didn't look at Paddy. She knew this was an ordeal she had to go through on her own, this assize of the night.

'I just like Paddy.'

'Good to you, is he? Buys you things? Nice silky stuff?'

'He's good to me.'

'Good to you. Any man would be good to the like of you. To the pretty little face on you. You might as well enjoy it. It all ends up the one way anyhow, you know that don't you?'

'I'm not sure.'

'You will be. Look at my husband. He's a fine man isn't he? Bear in mind he'd as lief kill you as look at you if you got in his way. He likes to get close up. That's what he told the man from the papers and that's what he does. Make sure the job is done right. He has as much conscience as that poker leaned against the fireplace there.'

'That's enough, Mary,' Dominic said.

'Just mind what I'm saying, girl, you seen nothing and heard nothing this night, you clear on that?'

'You'll scare the lassie to death,' Dominic said.

'I'm not scared,' Lorraine said.

'No, I can see that,' Mary said. 'I wonder why that is?' She came over to Lorraine and looked her in the eye.

'You should be scared. You must be accountable to man and you must be accountable to God.' Close up, Lorraine could see how a man could like Mary. There were something of death about her, a cold and damaged erotics which would take a man like a craving.

'You're just in time for the film show,' Mary said. Paddy looked at Lorraine and shrugged. Dominic drove a Land Rover up the kitchen window and attached leads to the battery to run the television. Lorraine wondered how they were going to watch a film and whether it would be some unholy epic of flesh and death for this was the place for it. But the film they watched was *The Right Stuff* about the first men sent into space which seemed to Lorraine to be about aloneness and apt to the high, remote country she found herself in. Dominic wanted to watch *Rio Grande* after that but Mary told him that he had left it late to put the geese in.

'The man who owns this house keeps geese,' Dominic said. 'We put them in at night.'

'I'll come with you,' Lorraine said. 'I like geese. I like animals.'

*

It was a starlit night, the moon near full, light coming off the galvanized farm roofs in radial glints and the wall stone frosted like quartz. She looked up to see if there were satellites, for the film had put her in mind of them, the spindly aerialled things.

The house was at the bottom of a high valley and the goose field was at the top. Dominic didn't speak as they walked. She knew that people called him Mad Dog although Paddy said that was only the newspapers and to pay no heed, but still. Dominic put his foot on a barred gate to climb it, then stopped. Lorraine could see white, unshaped objects on the field grass.

'We come a bit late for the geese.'

'Are they dead?'

'Some mink got in among them,' Dominic said. 'A fox'll kill just what it can eat. The mink, he kills the lot.' Dominic was at home in these high fields, these borderlands with the wild things, the blood drinkers. He climbed the gate and picked up a goose, holding it by the feet. There was a puncture wound in its neck.

'Still warm. I'd say the mink's in the wall there somewhere watching us.' She didn't like to think about them, these arcana of the night. The mink watching her now as she climbed the gate, the eyes glittering, constellated with yearning and their mouths still reddened, blood rosettes in the moonlight.

'Which one are you?' she said. 'The fox or the mink?'

'Maybe neither.'

Lorraine waited for fear to come, here in the presence of death with a man like Dominic, but the fear would not come. You felt you were cared for when you were with him. It was a quality he had. It wasn't goodness but it felt like something you might find in good people.

Paddy went outside to disconnect the battery lead. The Land Rover bonnet strut didn't work and Mary held the bonnet up for him.

'Are you not afraid for your girl up there with Dominic?'

'Are you not afraid for him?'

'You and your kind you're nothing but crooks but believe you me, something unholy is in that girl. She's a bad end waiting to happen.'

'We're all bad ends waiting to happen, Mary. You know that as well as I do.'

'You should take her away from this life.'

'I'll take her away when I can.'

'That's a lie and you know it but I'd treat her well if I was you.'

'I do treat her well Mary. You needn't fear for her.'

'It isn't her I fear for.'

There was a wayward power to Lorraine. Mary recognized a girl who would not be treated lightly. She had seen too many men like Paddy on the border. They were a ragged band and honourless, and their worth to themselves was measured solely in thievery and fraud. Courtship with such men was like being followed through darkened streets, footsteps gaining. Being a lover to one of them was like being stalked and caught and bundled into an alley,

When Dominic and Lorraine came back, Dominic gave Paddy a cardboard box containing the unsigned traveller's cheques he had come for. On their way out Dominic said for Lorraine to look after herself.

'Do you pray, Lorraine?' Mary said.

'I do.'

'Then pray for us all,' Mary said. Lorraine looked back at them as they drove off. Dominic and Mary stood in the doorway, Dominic's arm around Mary's shoulder, already faded and mythic through the frost-starred glass.

On the way home Lorraine brought Paddy to a small reservoir just off the main road at Ravensdale. An open gateway brought you to a pumping station and then the reservoir, the banked margins of it containing a round disc of still water. It was All Souls' Night, something turned adrift in the stillness and cold, condensed mist drifting inches deep on the surface of the water. Lorraine did not say anything to Paddy in case he laughed at her but All Souls was when the dead returned and she thought there was pale movement in the water mist and that those that were the lost, the undesired, stirred.

Lorraine told Jean that Dominic in the papers didn't look like he did in real life. He had a high forehead and receding hairline. A narrow moustache, well-trimmed, turning down either side of his mouth. In profile there was a bit of a jut to his chin, a fuck-you look, her mother called it. He had bone structure a woman would die for.

'Them eyes,' Jean said. 'I'd be scared to death if he ever even looked at me. I'd wet myself. It'd be running down my legs. Them's the eyes of a killer.'

'I kept seeing a reflection of myself in his eyes.'

'What reflection did you see?'

'I see a reflection of myself standing at my own grave weeping.'

'I see a reflection of me pissing myself laughing, catch yourself on, Lorraine.'

But the image would not leave Lorraine. A girl standing in a rained-on cemetery, wet earth piled high, mourners drifting away.

Out of the blue Paddy told Lorraine that he had looked through holiday brochures and that he was taking his wife on holiday.

'Where are you going?'

'Florida.'

'America.'

'That's right.'

'I don't even have a passport. I never even been out of the country.' Paddy laughed. 'Open the glove compartment.' Lorraine opened it and took out a bundle of Irish passports.

'Pick one.'

'You're laughing at me.' She took one of the green-bound passports in her hand.

'The cover is loose.'

'They were stolen from the bindery. They send them there to stitch the cover on. There's a boy there likes the ponies. He owed a few pound around the place.'

Lorraine remembered a young man she had seen with Paddy and Brendan in the foyer of the Imperial. The young man wearing a suit a size too big for him, hunched over, talking fast and moving his hands, there was something urgent he needed to get out there, something he needed to divest himself of, Brendan leaning back in his chair looking grave, his eyes on the young man's face as though urging him to revelation, Paddy looking off into the distance.

'And there's nothing wrote in them. No photographs or nothing.' Lorraine thought that the people who owned them had somehow been removed from the world and that their documents were all that was left of them, their ghosted remnants.

'They're blanks. Haven't been filled out yet.'

Lorraine turned on the interior light and held a page of the passport up against it.

'You could go to jail for this.'

'I been in jail.'

'What for?'

'Nothing.'

'They don't put you in jail for nothing.'

'They put me in jail for nothing. I was on remand. The judge says the police couldn't prove their case.'

'What did they say you done?'

'Money laundering.'

'What's that?' She thought of money hanging outside on a line, fresh-washed, whitened, although she knew it couldn't be that.

'If you got some cash and they don't like where you got it from, you have to change it into money you can use. Say you go to a car auction in England and buy an expensive motor with that cash and then you import it back across the border and get a new logbook for that car. Problem solved. You sell the car and put the money into the bank. The police says where did you get the money, you just say I sold my car.'

Lorraine knew there was more to it than that. The Bureau had something to do with it, there had been pieces in the newspaper about it and about Brendan and how he was in trouble with the law. Jean tried to show her the newspaper pieces but Lorraine refused to look. She liked the Brendan she knew and his talk of birds of prey and infra red and his expensive suits ruined with hard living, linens and tweed textured with spilled ash, cigarette burns on the cuffs.

Six

Brendan was always getting other people to sign official documents because he was bankrupt and wasn't allowed to sign them himself. Jean signed anyone's name on anything, it never cost her a thought even though Hutchie said she could get into trouble for it. Bann said Brendan wasn't allowed to have a bank account but what man devised God could put aside as long as it wasn't a sin.

Lorraine had heard people say that a man's word was his bond and she felt the same way about her signature. She'd practised signatures for hours on end when she was at school covering whole refill pads. She wanted to show herself as dependable but also capable of a wild heart. She kept the loops and flourishes for her first name. *Lorraine.* It was called after a place in France and she imagined quiet heat-struck streets in the daytime, an hotel with curtains moving a little in the breeze, Paddy lying beside her on a bed with tossed sheets and a sorrow she could not understand or resist, a felt sweetness in her mind. She said she wasn't going to just give all of that away by signing cheques or whatever it was Brendan wanted.

'I'll do anything you ask me to,' she said, 'but I don't have to do anything that Brendan asks me.'

'You don't have to do anything you don't want to,' Paddy said without looking at her. He didn't make a row out of it or anything which was worse and in the end she knew she would do it.

They spent the afternoon in the back room of the Bureau signing fake names on the American Express cheques and writing the numbers of the stolen passports on the back of each cheque. And when they were done Brendan took them to meet Owen Corrigan in the Sportsman's which was a modern bar and lounge two miles from the border. It was the place you ended up coming from matches, coming from the races, the place teeming on Saturday nights, close enough to the border to have that hinterland feel that the rules had changed, a codex of bad faith in place, everything expressed in glances and unfinished sentences.

Paddy liked the big new places like the Sportsman's, bars with carpeted floors. Paddy wasn't brash but he liked brash. He liked to be where money was being spent, good cars in the car park, the drinks more expensive, a wildness of new money in the air, people talking about the holidays they had in Spain and in Florida. Men with signet rings and sovereign medallions around their necks. They seemed to shimmer with a kind of foresight. Jean tried to act like one of their women all Gucci and knock-off Hermès pumps, but not a chance, they could see her for what she was.

'I like going out with Paddy,' Lorraine said.

'He brings you places like he won you or something,' Jean said.

'Won me like in a raffle? The pink ticket.'

'More like one of them car raffles.'

'What sort of car would I be? Something good. A Ferrari maybe.'

'No. Nothing as good as that.'

Lorraine disliked Corrigan from the minute she met him. There were men like him everywhere, all glancing touches and suggestive remarks. Detective Inspector Owen Corrigan wore pink shirts and white linen jackets with a handkerchief in the breast pocket. He liked to be seen at the races and at the courthouse in Dundalk when the television cameras were there and at extradition handovers on the border at Killeen. Corrigan took three foreign holidays a year and golfed in Florida. He had a camel overcoat draped over his shoulders and wore tinted glasses and walked the streets of Dundalk like he was in a fucking film, Hutchie said, greeting people, working the street, all guardian of the law bonhomie when he was on the fix morning, noon and night. He had accumulated multiple properties in the town and in Drogheda. He regarded himself as a sportsman and was seen at the races and at the greyhounds at Dundalk greyhound track.

Hutchie said Corrigan took part in dogfights and at cockfights in North Louth farm sheds. Jean could not abide the idea of animals being made to fight each other for sport and that men made and lost thousands. Eamon said it was just nature and the dogs and roosters were born to it and would pine and die unless they fought.

'I hope the police find them,' Jean said.

'Corrigan is the fucking police,' Hutchie said.

'God bless the poor dogs and roosters,' Bann said.

'Those men should be locked up.'

'Not much hope of that,' Eamon said. 'If you want to go you're sent from one place to another and each time a man meets you and sends you on another crooked mile. You could be roaming half the night before you get there. Police would never find them even if they wanted to.'

Lorraine thought that Corrigan looked like a sinister man from a film with the glasses that went dark in sunlight. He kept new banknotes in a leather wallet and fanned them out on hotel tables. She knew that Brendan liked to gamble and Corrigan talked about casinos in Florida and Cuba and said that someone like Lorraine could get a job there as a hostess in a casino no bother. She wondered who this Lorraine might be, in stockings and basque, a worldly, burnished quality to her, conducting knowing conversations with men in velour banquettes. That night she lay awake in her bedroom in Boyle O'Reilly Terrace, the floodlights of the Lourdes stadium casting shadows on her ceiling.

Lorraine told Nora she believed in religious relics like the mitt of Padre Pio, which was a kind of saint's glove which travelled about the country healing people. Nora knew that she was serious and wouldn't laugh at her. Lorraine said she often prayed at the shrine to Blessed Oliver Plunkett in St Peter's church across the road from Boyle O'Reilly Terrace. Plunkett had been hanged, drawn and quartered three hundred years before and his head afterwards enshrined as a relic, a dark leathery thing, bag-like. She wondered about remnants in the brain case, something fibrous, she thought, knotted and dusty and beyond dreaming.

She couldn't tell Paddy about these things though he never said anything about the scapulars she wore around her neck or that she turned the plastic Virgin Mary from Lourdes to the wall when they were in bed together. Sometimes she remembered when she was little she would kneel at the side of her bed in her cotton nightgown and say her prayers, and sometimes even now with Paddy sleeping beside her she would whisper to herself *Now I lay me down to sleep I pray the Lord my soul to keep, May the angels watch me through the night and keep me in their blessed sight.*

Corrigan would flirt with Nora. A lot of men did, market traders from Jonesborough and from Newry market. Sometimes they'd bring her a gift from the market stall, a carriage clock or a poinsettia. Nora seemed to enjoy their attention, these down at heel gallants in slip-on shoes and check jackets. They'd croon Sammy Davis Junior or Sinatra numbers through cigarette smoke and offer to take her to old time dances in broken-down lounge bars in the suburbs. They'd be on their best manners with Nora, no off-colour remarks. They knew breeding when they saw it and Jean had told them about Nora being a debutante in the time of dance cards and girls who wore fascinators and satin gloves to their elbows. Corrigan was the only man who would actually take hold of her and waltz her around the office, the reek of Denim aftershave off him fit to knock you down, Jean said, but Nora didn't seem to mind.

'If he took them kind of liberties with me, he'd soon know about it,' Jean said.

'There's no harm in it,' Lorraine said, 'and Nora gets a laugh out of it.' But when Corrigan was dancing with Nora his eyes would still follow Lorraine and Lorraine knew that for some men harm was all there was.

When Paddy went to a cockfight Lorraine came with him. She didn't think Paddy had any interest in bloodsports but he said it was business. They drove up through Culloville past the garage offering cut-price diesel and past the electrical goods stores priced for both sides. You didn't know what side of the border you were on. You weren't supposed to know. This was border locale subject to border law. They drove to a phone box outside Culloville, a drizzle coming down and the phone box light shorted and flickering. Paddy waited inside the phone box until a call came through directing him to a border crossing. The crossing had been cratered by soldiers but the craters had been filled in and Paddy was able to drive over it. At the far end a man with a baseball cap over his eyes sent them further into border country, down an overgrown road, briars and dog rose dragging on the side of the car. They came to galvanized shedding, painted with red lead. The laneway to it had been reinforced with hardcore and broken stone and there were jeeps and Hiaces lined along the north side of it where they couldn't be seen from any of the hillside observation posts. You can hear dogs somewhere close by, there's a lonesome baying.

A narrow corridor has been made down the outside of the shed, pipework and ducting running along it. Something ominous in the air, ill-lit and troubling. Scuffling in the wetted sand. The handlers stroke the roosters' feathers and pull their beaks, raise their hackles, bind stainless steel gaffs to their legs, show them to each other, there's a smell of fresh blood in the air, a taint, you can't be in here and believe in anything any more, powerful carbide lights hung over the ring so that it is shadowless.

'You alright being here?'

'I wouldn't be here if I minded it,' Lorraine said. Brendan and Corrigan were seated on hay bales the far side of the ring, Brendan intent, his glasses glinting in the light looking like this was happening because he had ordained it. Corrigan leaned back so that his face was in the shadow, but Lorraine could feel his eyes on her, Corrigan always watching, and she knew he knew what he was thinking. That look Corrigan had. It was like hands all over you. Lorraine knowing that she was the only woman in the shed and that carried eerie power in this place of blood and yearning. Paddy went over to the ring. Lorraine saw the young man who had sold Paddy the passports. His hair was lank and fell over his forehead and there was a tear in his trouser leg over the knee. The handlers released the cocks and they circled each other in the ring. Paddy took a roll of notes held with a rubber band and put it in the inner pocket of the young man's jacket.

*

In the car Lorraine spat on a tissue. There was a fine spray of blood on Paddy's face and collar and she wiped it off.

'You didn't mind it?' Paddy said.

'No, I didn't mind it. I could take that shirt back with me and wash the blood out of the collar.'

'Am I supposed to go about with no shirt on me?'

'I don't mind.'

'I have to go,' Paddy said. 'I'll drop you home.'

'Take me to the carriage,' Lorraine said, 'and then you can go wherever you're going.'

Seven

Lorraine liked Eamon. There was an openness about him, a big-man lavishness, he gave you the feeling that his physical presence was something gifted on you. Two weeks after they had signed the American Express cheques they were watching the Grand National in the Sportsman's and she had ten pounds on Rough Quest that Brendan had bet for her. The punters were on their feet and shouting at the television and she couldn't see over their heads. She felt hands around her waist and then Eamon had lifted her into the air so that she could see the television. None of the rest of them would have thought to do it and she saw Corrigan looking at her with a sour puss on him but Eamon held her like she was fragile.

Eamon danced with her that evening. Paddy didn't dance at discos but Eamon said Paddy went line dancing on a Saturday night. When Lorraine danced with Eamon she could see the white of his smile in the disco light but there was nothing else in it and when it came to a slow dance he led her off the floor. 'A Whiter Shade of Pale' was playing. Eamon was watching someone, a young man in a white shirt and a black waistcoat at the edge of the dance floor.

'Fucking Colm McKevitt,' Jean said. 'Like he owns the place.' McKevitt walked towards their table. He was pale with dark hair and darting eyes, something thievish about him, he'd be light-fingered around your good intentions.

'Watch your handbag when he's around,' Jean said.

'Does he steal stuff?' Lorraine said.

'Anything that's not nailed down,' Eamon said.

'He'd steal you right out of your knickers,' Jean said. Lorraine half knew what she meant. He wasn't goodlooking but he had a heretical allure. He stopped in front of Lorraine and nodded towards the dance floor.

'She's not dancing,' Eamon said.

'She danced with you didn't she?'

'But she's not fucking dancing with you, McKevitt.'

'I can speak for myself,' Lorraine said, but she wasn't really annoyed. She felt safe with Eamon and she knew that the conversation wouldn't go beyond uncivil exchanges. Not this time anyway.

'Paddy'll be back in a minute,' Hutchie said, 'so take yourself off.'

'So this is Farrell's woman,' McKevitt said. Lorraine sipped at her drink and said nothing, and he smiled in what was meant to be a meaning way.

'What are you doing with border trash like Paddy Farrell? Unless you're trash yourself.'

Lorraine had met men more dangerous than McKevitt, who knew what there was to be known about taking, nothing behind their eyes. Men who could empty you out. They spoke and their hands made hollowed-out gestures. Men who thought themselves entitled to your substance, who could sup from what you were. Not McKevitt who wanted to get you onto the dance floor so he could feel you up or some other low-level pilferage of self that she had long since stopped caring about.

Certain desires got to run unchecked in the border country. What you coveted you took. The border lured people into doing things that otherwise they would have known to leave well alone. Colm McKevitt elsewhere would have been a small-town hoodlum running wild for a few years. There would be court appearances for petty crime, pub fights, drink driving. He would have pulled himself together in his early twenties. But McKevitt had grown a meanness in himself that would not go away. He had carried out robberies in the border area and the hinterland towns. There would be killing next and in the meantime there was breaking into people's homes and hijacking. He wanted to be Dominic but McGlinchey knew that every operation he carried out was an elaboration of his own legend and he was detailed and ruthless in everything he did. You needed to be epic in those years and McKevitt wasn't. McKevitt just did the next thing. And that was what got you killed.

Paddy went to Florida that August and when he came back he looked different. Sunstruck. Lorraine had never seen him with a tan before. He looked like he had been in a good land. When she held him she could smell suncream. Paddy was always small-town formal in matters of dress, jeans, polished brogues, open neck shirt and sports jacket. Lorraine liked to walk barefoot at home but Paddy didn't take his shoes off. She tried to imagine him in shorts and a polo shirt and thought the image diminished him. She thought of him in pastels and beach things in the sunshine, a man paraded in front of himself, a carnival made of him. The clothes he wore every day were fitted, some purpose to them, the male part of him contained. Then when it came off the nakedness of him surprised you every time, a man standing in front of you nude and revealed, the pale limbed thing given to you alone.

Eight

When Lorraine was nine she wrote a book in school. It was called Lorraine by Lorraine. The teacher asked them to pick a confirmation name. They were supposed to pick a grandparent's name or a family name, something handed down through the years, the name of a favourite teacher or a saint. When the teacher asked her what name she had chosen Lorraine said please miss I chose Destiny. Afterwards it was a family story and everyone laughed but Lorraine could not see why people laughed. She thought it was a right thing that you could see from a young age that your fate was written in the stars for all to see.

In school they learned about the boy prince Tutankhamun and how before they buried him in the pyramids they removed his organs and placed them in jars. The heart, the liver, the kidneys packaged in leaves. The brain was removed by a hook which was inserted into the skull-pan through the nostrils. She would lie awake at night and think about the centuries passing and the boy prince in his embalmed darkness.

Paddy was always talking about leaving his wife at the start. How men talk. Those lonely words. Lorraine felt for the wife. They could be like sisters given a chance. She thought about the phone ringing, Hi it's me Lorraine they would talk sister things, breathy confidences, the voice lowered.

'Men all talk like that,' Jean said. 'They're all leaving the wife at the start.' Lorraine said this is different. There is that shared name. They were both called Farrell and the bloodlines must meet somewhere. On some level they are blood relatives.

'That's against the law,' Jean said.

'Don't spoil things,' Lorraine said. But it was true that some part of her could feel the taint, deep in the blood.

After Paddy came back from Florida he set up Lorraine in a flat in Newry close to the Buttercrane Quay. Lorraine didn't know if Paddy owned the flat but she did know that he had some sort of interest in the hotel opposite. She met Hutchie in Soho car park. She parked the Peugeot beside Hutchie's E-Class and said, 'Nice motor, Hutchie,' only meaning it as a compliment but Hutchie thought she was talking down to him and asked her what it was like to be a kept woman.

'Prick,' Jean said, 'I wouldn't listen to the one-eyed bastard, he has a face on him like a cat's arse.'

'Corrigan called as well. Said he wanted to wish me well in my new place.'

'Thon slippy cunt,' Jean said. 'No harm to you, my love, he never wished well to anyone save his bank account in all his born days.'

'You know where Paddy takes the wife?' Corrigan had said.

'It's none of my business.'

'It's all of your business, girl. He takes her to the Roadhouse on a Saturday night and they have a steak dinner and then they go line dancing in Lacey's. Paddy says it's full of young ones but she likes it so he goes along with it.'

Corrigan knew what he was doing with Lorraine. He told Hutchie *I set her going like a watch, the fucking tramp.* On Saturday night Lorraine drove to the Roadhouse through the townlands of Ballymascanlon and Annavernagh. She parked at the far corner of the car park to watch them going in. Paddy was driving a silver Lexus with Dublin plates. His wife got out of the car first and stood waiting for him, then she walked in front to the door of the hotel. Paddy held it open for her, a regular Saturday night gallant, Lorraine thought. The wife wore a blue frock and Lorraine wondered if he had zipped her into it, his breath on the nape of her neck.

*

The car park and entrance to the Roadhouse could be seen from the army surveillance post on the low mountain ridge to the west of the main border crossing. The post was an armoured container mounted on metal scaffold poles. The military employed infra-red cameras and enhanced night-vision scopes to surveil the road network and fields of their border sector. The stunted mountain foxes took prey in the lower slopes and they barked icy messages to each other in the frozen valleys. It was a time of the watchful, and espionage and desire sometimes ran together.

It was cold in the Roadhouse car park and Lorraine thought about walking into the hotel dining room and telling Paddy she loved him in front of his wife but her nose was streaming and confronting a wife with snot running down her chin did not appeal. But she wanted Paddy. She wanted wildness. She could see Paddy and her in pursuit across open country, every hand turned against them. Every door barred apart from the few who were willing to take a risk on their outlaw allure. She would take Paddy's arm and put her head on his shoulder. If he looked down he would see her face softened in the dashboard lights, bound to him in backlit fidelities, the radio talking about events along the border, road closures, hijacked cars, driving past the filling stations and bureaus de change on the northern side, everything bootleg and tawdry, they're putting industrial alcohol in Smirnoff bottles and selling it round the pubs, they're cooking the trace dye out of diesel oil, bringing it across the border in tankers. Nobody is saying that the customs are paid off but they are. This is the most highly surveilled area of Europe, there are military watchtowers, continuous helicopter overflights, Lynx choppers coming in from Bessbrook airbase, you don't land you hover, and foot patrols fall to the ground and they're seen if they're seen at all as grainy, running shapes, these are the invoked phantoms of the drop zone. Eamon can drive a forty ton rigid tanker of doctored diesel oil along the border and make it disappear. There are sheds which straddle the borderline, and there are tunnels, and who's to say that the truck you drive in one end is the truck that you drive out the other end?

This is strange terrain, unsolid, ghosted through.

When she got back to the car Eamon was waiting for her. He was wearing a green velvet jacket and jeans.

'You know that Paddy seen you when he was going in? He rung me.' Lorraine couldn't understand how Paddy had seen her.

'You don't get it,' Eamon said. 'Paddy's always three steps ahead. He knew you were going to be there before the thought come into your mind.'

'What did he say?' Lorraine said. Paddy had told Eamon to get her the fuck out of there, that he was out with his wife but Eamon said that Paddy didn't want her getting frozen standing out in the cold and that she had to trust him.

'You don't have to lie to me Eamon, but thank you. You look like you're going dancing?'

'Ballymartin marquee.'

'Can I come with you?'

'If you get the snot off your face'

They drove along the northern side of Carlingford Lough, the borderline running down the centre of the shipping channel, the lock gates and canal no longer used, through the port of Warrenpoint and Rostrevor. They passed the bombed and burned-out shells of the Roxboro and Great Northern hotels, gaunt and sentinel on the landside and mid-channel also sentinel a British Navy corvette. It lacked insignia and there was no nameplate or serial number on the bow. The Haulbowline light swept over it and for a moment you could see in detail the dented plates, sealed portholes, greyish-white paintwork, a ghost ship in the carbide beam. The corvette was moored to a fixed buoy on the northern side of the deepwater channel. Soldiers embarked from it in rigid inflatables, stopped and searched shipping on the lough. At night on the shoreline you could hear the radios, the marine band chatter over the mudflats and bents.

There were signs for Rathfriland and Hilltown and they went by Mill Bay and into Kilkeel. Past the curlew beds and mudflats, the lights of Greenore docks on the other side, the gantry lights of laden tankers awaiting high tide outside the bar. On the outskirts of Kilkeel they passed roadside gospel halls and Pentecostalists in their Sunday suits and their wives in headscarves. They wanted to be known as lost peoples. You looked up at night and saw their house lights in the distance, scattered on the mountainside. Lorraine said why don't we stop and talk to them. But Eamon told her to cut the holy talk and not to go next nor near them or he'd throw her out by the side of the road and leave her there and see how she got on as a strange girl cast up outside their corrugated tin halls.

'Someone like you would appear among them like the devil himself,' Eamon said. For Satan was known to speak in womanish tones. As well as that some months before a gospel hall had been riddled with fire from assault rifles, one of which had been traced to Dominic's band. Lorraine went quiet at that. They'd covered five or six miles before she spoke.

'Fox or mink,' Lorraine said.

'What's that?'

'It's what Dominic said to me. We were up the mountain and these geese were killed and he told me how a fox would kill one but a mink would kill all.'

'I'd say Dominic is both the fox and the mink and see no differ to tell you the truth.'

Eamon took a half-bottle of crème de menthe from the glove compartment and offered it to her. She'd never had it before and found it sickly but took a mouthful. 'Seems like round here they like their drinks sweet and their women sweeter.' She drawled the line mock cowboy and she could see Eamon smiling in the dashboard light.

'Listen,' Eamon said, 'you need to leave it be. Paddy and the wife. That's always going to be there. You're only making things bad for yourself by thinking different.' She liked Eamon for trying. You got the feeling that he was on your side.

That was the mistake she made. Nobody was on anyone's side.

The marquee was pitched on a field north of Ballymartin. In the gathering dusk you would have thought it one of the tent missions erected in the summer months for itinerant evangelicals and Pentecostalists preaching the light that shone from within. Up close though it felt like an old-time travelling show, it had that edge of town carny feel to it. There would be a freak show out back, something caged, something whimpering in the straw. Eamon pulled up in a field car park and they walked up the path towards the tent, coloured bulbs strung from trees on the approach. Eamon paid for both of them at the door.

The look was cowboy, cast as mythic, their landscapes haunted. Men and women who saw rawhide versions of their lives in the westerns showing in the Vogue in Kilkeel, the Frontier cinema in Newry. The music was country. Solo singers and travelling showbands with hard-eyed female leads. The Dixies,

The Hilton. Troubadours in frilled shirts and velvet jackets. Prairie mystique was what the crowd wanted and paid for at the door. The punters wore rhinestone-studded cowboy boots and satin blouses with western ties and they jived to the sobbed-out tales of poverty and loss. Fights were frequent. They felt they owed it to the cowboy mystiques they brought, that they were red-eyed hands just come off the trail and working off long lonely nights under a range moon. They grappled with each other across the dance floor, the crowd scattering. There were factions that ran through this country, loyalty demanded violence and all understood it, men stripped to the waist with knuckles bloodied and opened to the bone. Eamon led Lorraine onto the floor. The slow sets were waltzed and they jived the fast ones, dust spurting up from the raised plank dance floor, skirts flaring. Speedy Fegan was the only man in the hall wearing trainers and Eamon beckoned him over.

'I hear you're the coming man Fegan.'

'You don't let the grass grow under your feet yourself, Eamon.'

'I fucking hope you're not here doing business.'

'Move over, big dog. I'm here for the Hank Williams, Eamon. I'm not plying my evil trade in these here parts if that's what you mean though. The schoolchildren and housewives are safe from me, safe as houses.' Speedy talking too fast and grinding his teeth in a way that Lorraine didn't understand. Speedy was one of those people that were described as hard to dislike but Lorraine felt there was wrongness in him. He was also described as someone who would come to a bad end, which was true.

'Maybe I believe you,' Eamon said, 'for you'll sell no drugs here, Speedy.'

'Not tonight, Eamon, but I'm the coming man, born slippy. Move over big dog.'

Lorraine didn't know how to jive but Eamon took the lead. He was a good dancer for a big man, he had a loose wrist action. You knew Eamon wasn't going to let you go, that you wouldn't go spinning off into the other dancers. Afterwards Lorraine told Jean that she liked a man she could trust and Jean laughed.

'You're in the wrong place for trust my love. I wouldn't trust a man jack of them.'

'Not that sort of trust,' Lorraine said. She meant the kind of man who would leave you home without hands everywhere and would sit with his arm around you with music playing on the radio.

They left the marquee at half past two and drove back across the border and had chips and burgers at the van in the square in Dundalk. The chip vans had been there for decades and there were signed postcards yellowed and curling from showbands of another era pinned to the chipboard above the worker's heads, men in bow ties and shirts with frills, women with beehives and false eyelashes, and they made Lorraine feel sad for these lost bandsmen coiffed and smiling as though a long time ago things were different and these lost troubadours attested to it. The thought of them and of the young Elvis made a tear come to her eye and she asked Eamon to play Elvis. Eamon only had early songs, 'Hound Dog' and 'Jailhouse Rock', but really she liked the sad Elvis, the overweight one in Graceland's lonely rooms, the adrift and ill-starred fat boy. She thought she could sit and talk to him and afterwards she would take him by the hand and lead him back to the place of all his yearning, the dirt roads and clapboard churches and backwoods croonings in the years of his making.

Eamon took her to the Flagstaff viewpoint above Newry to see the sun rise. From the Flagstaff you looked down the lough, past the lights of Warrenpoint on the north shore and Greenore on the southern shore and the mountain ranges behind each port, the entrance to the lough being the gap between the mountain ranges, open to the sea, open to the world, the border running down the centre of the navigation channel and out to sea until it was lost in the vastness beyond.

Young men and women were on the move coming from Lacey's and the Imperial, from the Border Inn and the Ballymac. You find them parked in these neglected beauty spots and weed-grown car parks. The car seats are nubbed plastic and leave an imprint on bare skin when the girls have been laid down in the backseat. At first light you find the girls hunched down in the passenger seats, smoking, a boy's jacket pulled round their bare shoulders, pale heiresses of the dawn.

'I got a run to do,' Eamon said.

'What do you mean, a run?' Lorraine said.

'It's no good being an innocent around here, you know that?'

'You know they always say I'm not as innocent as I look.'

'Hard to say on the evidence, Lorraine.'

'Maybe you're looking in the wrong place.'

'Maybe I am.'

Eamon's diesel laundering plant was located in a semi-derelict farmyard on the southern side of the border. A shipping container had been buried in the ground and the plant had been built inside it. You had to go down a steel ladder to get in. The plant was lit by bulkhead lights, diesel was pumped from a road tanker above ground into a silage tank raised on blocks in the middle of the bunker. Heavy-duty cabling hung in coils from the ceiling. Condensation ran down the concrete walls. The pumps were running from a generator, the noise ear-splitting in the underground bunker and the exhaust fumes of the generator hung blue in the air. There were spilled polythene bags of Fuller's earth piled against the wall, the floor sticky with contaminants. It was hard to breathe but the two men working the plant did not notice. The smell of diesel and exhaust fumes stayed on her skin for weeks.

'There's a run ready to go,' Eamon said. They went back up the stepladder to the hay barn concealing the entrance to the bunker. He handed out walkie-talkies to a group of young men and made them test them. They were veteran to this.

The diesel run. 8.15 a.m. Cloud banks low over Gullion mountain. Drizzle hanging in the bare alder and ash branches. The ditches are hacked back to widen the road and the gash marks are vivid white as though white roses bloomed in the stour and damp of a winter's morning.

The high corrugated gates to the yard are held in place by steel posts. There are three spotter cars, Datsuns and Escorts with lowered suspensions and body kits, waiting outside the gate. The drivers have baseball caps pulled down over their eyes and walkie-talkies. They're all wearing overalls. They drive in convoy to the first junction. The Datsun stays there and the Escorts split off to stop at the next crossroads. They will patrol crossroads to crossroads. The risen sun is bronze behind leaden clouds.

The marker dye has been stripped out of the diesel oil and it is time to deliver it to stations in the border counties and beyond. Eight diesel tankers start up and the gates are opened. The engines are loud, the drivers revving them and slipping them into gear. That's the sound of fucking money, Eamon said, but Lorraine thought it hard not to believe that some mayhem beyond the making of money is involved in this. Harm breeds harm and all hearts are now corrupted, the roads themselves are corpse grounds. Walkie-talkie crackle, a diesel lorry changing down gears, sweet border anthems.

'You can't be following Paddy like that,' Jean said. 'And you need to stop being jealous.'

'He likes me jealous.'

'Not when you're dragging up stuff from years ago and throwing it in his face and following him around when he's with his wife and nagging him.'

'I don't nag.'

'You don't think you nag but that look in your eyes is nagging, that and the little voice you put on. Men get sick of that brave and quick.'

'You think he's the type of man gets tired of a girl and moves on to the next one?'

'Every man's that type of man, are you stupid or something? You start out at the sex stage,' Jean said, 'and now you've gone on to the homey stage.'

'What's the next stage?' Lorraine said but Jean just made a face and said you'll find out.

Nine

Brendan had defrauded his client accounts and been struck off in the High Court in Belfast. He could no longer practise as a lawyer. That March he was summonsed to Newry Courthouse and charged with fraud. He was given bail and the file was sent to the DPP. They went to the Hermitage on Canal Street close to the courthouse to wait for Brendan but he didn't turn up.

'Struck off is not enough for them,' Jean said. 'The peelers is after him now for fraud. What did his poor wife do to deserve that?' Lorraine wanted to know why the police were after Brendan since he was so friendly with Corrigan. Jean said that there were different types of police and that besides Corrigan was from the other side of the border. There was the police who arrested criminals and gave you speeding tickets and then there was the police of the shadows and those were the ones that Brendan was friendly with.

'Can they not get rid of the fraud charges though?' Lorraine said. Jean said no. Every badness had its boundaries and if you strayed beyond them you were on your own.

'Brendan'll get out of it,' Hutchie said.

'How the fuck is he going to do that?' Jean said.

'Quis custodiet ipsos custodes?' Hutchie said.

'What sort of up my hole gaolhouse cant is that for fuck's sakes?' Jean said.

'Who judges the judge?' Hutchie said.

'He's drunk,' Jean said, 'he doesn't know what it means. He picked it up from sitting in court waiting for his seven years' hard.'

'Look at everyone you know in the bar,' Hutchie said. 'Who would you want to be your judge? Who would you want to stand over you?'

'Judged for what?' Jean said. 'I wouldn't let a man jack of them empty my bins, never mind judge me.'

'For things you haven't done yet but you're going to do.'

'What are you saying to me? I never done nothing.'

'Everybody's done something.'

Lorraine thought that her sins were women's sins, those of despising your own quality, of infidelity to self, of the good in you unmade. There was not a man standing who could sit in judgement over women's things but if she was made to choose she would say Brendan.

'Why?' She didn't have the words to say Brendan knew that remorse was present in the world even if he would never avail of it so she said nothing.

'I wouldn't pick none of this crew for they'd walk away without a backward glance, lock, stock and barrel.'

'Why do you always talk around corners, Hutchie?'

'What I'm trying to say is that Brendan has his own pet judge. Alcoholic by the name of Mr Justice Cecil Hearty, and Brendan owes him. Him and Brendan's big pals from way back. Brendan's trying to bide his time until Hearty comes up on the judges' list and he'll drop the charges. That's why he's not here. He's drinking with Hearty.'

'So there's no problem.'

'There is. There's plenty lawyers don't like when one of their own goes rogue. They can't do nothing about Hearty, but they can do something about Brendan. He won't get another remand and they're lining up another judge that'll put him away for good and all.'

They found Brendan later that night. Brendan went to the dark bars, the old bars. The place he went to most was McCrink's in a row of houses which was all that was left when the new road was built, the render all cracked, the roof plates sunk. It was a drinkers' bar. There was no sign on the front to say what it was, you had to know it was there and that was what Brendan liked about it. He liked knowing things that no one else knew and he liked to be with these people who all looked spent in the daylight but reached some edge-of-dying glamour at night, the men in threadbare suits and their small hollow-cheeked women wearing lipstick ten shades too red and drinking Babycham like they were weaning themselves away from the habits of living. Why would you dress up to come to a bar like this, Lorraine asked Paddy and he said it was like the way people put on glad rags to go to a funeral.

You knew when Brendan was meeting Judge Cecil Hearty in a bar because the judge's close protection detail would be outside, two plainclothes detectives in a parked car. That was how they tracked him down. Brendan and the judge were sitting at the back on an old bus seat with tears in the fabric, the two men side by side both drunk, the judge jowly and dissolute, staring at those who came and went with ruined hauteur.

'He looks like a boy who'd have the hand out for a bribe,' Hutchie said. Outside he smiled at the two plainclothes men, a lopsided provoking grimace. The police knew what Hutchie was and he knew what they were.

'Don't be riling them,' Bann said. The driver rolled down his window.

'What are you smiling at, Hutchie, you half-blind bastard?

Look at me like that again and I'll pull the other eye out of your head.'

'You haven't done it yet.'

'Leave them be,' Bann said. There was a tired feel to the dialogue, a feel of half-hearted beatings in basement cells, jaded interrogations.

At the end of the night the bar emptied, but Brendan and Judge Cecil Hearty sat on side by side mindlessly drunk and unspeaking. The two policemen entered and brought them out. Jean didn't know what transaction took place between Brendan and the judge and she knew not to ask. Nora said they were old friends and had been to university together.

The night before Brendan was next due in court Lorraine accompanied Paddy to the Bureau. Paddy took a phial of clear liquid from the attaché case and gave it to Brendan. Paddy said that Brendan needed an excuse not to turn up in court the following day because the judge was hostile. The liquid in the phial was supposed to cause symptoms similar to that of appendicitis. Brendan was told to take a sip but he drank it all. He was taken to Daisy Hill Hospital by ambulance that night and Owen accompanied him.

'He must have been in some pain,' Hutchie said. 'Ambulance man told me you could hear him screeching three streets away.'

Owen had sat with his screaming father until the dawn broke and the effect of the drug wore off. The hospital provided

Brendan with a letter for the court excusing him from attending on medical grounds and he was granted a further remand, but it came at a price. Nora saw Owen on the street later that day. He walked as if he was blown by a strange wind and he was bone-white with the grief of it. How the fathers howl in the night of their pain and demand the ruin of their sons.

The meeting with Hearty wasn't just about the charges against Brendan. Three weeks later Paddy told Lorraine that Brendan had taken a case against American Express and had gone to the High Court in Belfast.

'Why are you suing American Express? They were the ones got robbed,' Lorraine said.

'There's a bit more to it than that.'

'If you tell me not to bother my pretty little head, if you even think it –' She made a girl fist under his nose. Mock tough was as far as you got to go with Paddy, sometimes not even that far. Not that he would hit you, more that there was something there that had to be kept under control and you had to help him do it. He was a man out alone in the bleak ranges of his calling. There was an abundance there but also a danger. But he never even raised his voice to her. You had to respect that.

American Express had refused to pay out on the traveller cheque transactions and Brendan brought them to the High Court in

Belfast to order the release of the funds. Counsel for both sides knew that the transaction was fraudulent, for how could they not have known, but without evidence and in the knowledge that procedure had been followed in the cashing of the cheques Judge Cecil Hearty said that he had no choice but to find for Brendan.

To complete the Amex operation the bank draft made out in payment by court order had to be exchanged for used notes and distributed among the players. Brendan knew that the Bank of Ireland in Dundalk kept stocks of used sterling banknotes and was anxious to exchange them. The court case had attracted publicity. Anyone with any wit would know that the money would be converted into cash and put into circulation on the border. Several nights running a car followed Brendan home. The road to Ravensdale went by the forest margin, and at night mist filled the bottom of the valley so that it was hard to make out distant headlights in your rear-view mirror or to separate them from other border wraiths and visions but after the fourth time it happened Brendan spoke to Corrigan. Corrigan said that it was likely Colm McKevitt.

Brendan had to do the bank run, Brendan alone had reason to be on the road with large sums of money, and if Paddy was stopped by police, customs or army, the money's provenance would be questioned at best, confiscated at worst. Hutchie could not be trusted. Corrigan confirmed that Colm McKevitt had heard that a large amount of cash was to cross the border, and if McKevitt knew then so did others, for McKevitt was also a mouth. Then there was the McGlincheys. They had fulfilled their part of the deal and the money was now back in circulation and could be legitimately stolen again.

Paddy left a Mercedes 320SL outside the Bureau, keys on the driver's side front tyre under the wheel arch. Brendan got into it and started it and waited for Jean and Owen to get in. Jean to make them look like husband and wife on a shopping trip not felons working on completion of a job involving kidnapping, extortion and fraud. Owen to sit in the back of the car to count the bundles of cash. Brendan drove the Mercedes as he drove other cars, almost absent, outside himself. Jean thought it was a lovely car but to Brendan it was just a tool to do a job. Twenty years old or brand new like this one. It didn't bother him.

She had asked Hutchie how much a car like that cost but Hutchie had just smiled.

'Car like that's cheap. You just have to sell your soul.'

'Would you not answer one question straight in your life, you one-eyed fucker,' she said.

She hoped that she was seen going through Newry in the Mercedes by some of her friends. She knew that Brendan was tainted by bankruptcy and fraud proceedings but still to be seen driving with him in a fancy motor would shorten their cough, fixing her make-up in the backlit vanity mirror built in above her eyeline.

They weren't stopped at the military checkpoint at Cloghogue and crossed the border at the customs plaza, lorries queued on the hard shoulder to present their documents. The border hauliers. The big Scanias ticking over, diesel smoke hanging in the air. Hiace and Commer vans. Men standing talking or queuing for the customs hut with papers in their hands, she's thinking of a bazaar, a trading post somewhere far off. There's always someone to motion you down a back alley. There's always a deal to be done.

Brendan staying in the traffic, driving easy on the way down, a Silk Cut burning in the ashtray. Getting faster as they got close. He wasn't saying much but Jean was happy to sit back and feel the kick of the engine in her back as he went down through the gears, the eight cylinder jolt and hum, the road widening, entering Dundalk past the graveyard and the yards of the customs agents, Jean caught up in the exalted rush, Owen in the back not speaking. They drove past the bank. Brendan pulled into the car park of a pub with rusting cartwheels and fake timbering on the walls. Jean said nothing. She was used to being places like this with men like Brendan, empty car parks and laybys, out on the margins, places set aside to remind you about lonesomeness and failed promise. There was nothing to do but wait. Brendan put a Perry Como cassette in the deck. She wondered how he could be both things, here with the engine off, cigarette ash spilled on his linen suit, cuffs and seams frayed, his face at rest, grey and tired, at times a ragged phantom and at times you could see the mind on fire.

An Escort pulled up beside them and a bank clerk got out. You could tell that he didn't like what he was doing, that he did not see his job as being carried out in a car park, transferring canvas bags of used notes between cars, Owen counting the bundles. The manager looked at Brendan and knew he came from disorder and wished him to return to it, the woman sitting in the passenger seat the type you'd edge up to at the end of the night knowing your disappointment would be safe with her.

The bank clerk filled the back of the car with bags of cash and left without speaking. Brendan started the Mercedes and pulled out, Owen starting to count. Jean looked behind her and saw a police motorcycle. The motorcycle tried to overtake them on the bridge over the Fane river but Brendan dropped down through the gears and accelerated away pushing the speed, hitting ninety, cars getting out of their way, the drivers trying to catch a glimpse of the passengers, Jean thinking celebrity or notoriety not caring which. They swept through the outskirts of Dundalk, and onto the open road. Jean saw that the outrider could not catch them, the Mercedes speedometer over 110 now, the motorcycle cop falling back, flattening himself over the petrol tank to cut down the wind but still losing the big car. It seemed to her that Brendan was writing some legend of himself, that since he had lost the status that came with being a lawyer he sought another way to attract regard, and was in fact exalted, written in the same border annals as Dominic and Paddy and others.

They passed through the outskirts of Dundalk, the outrider long gone, and then they were entering the forest at Ravensdale approaching the customs, the road in shadow, Brendan driving down the white line so that lorries and cars coming the other way had to pull into the hard shoulder. Brendan went through the customs post without slowing down and the pursuit was picked up by the police on the northern side of the border.

Jean saw the armoured police Cortina come up behind them, the road too busy for the police to overtake, the police car's ballistic windscreen glass greenish and opaque so you couldn't see who was inside. Despite the underbody plating and armour it was able to keep up with the Mercedes. She tried to catch Owen's eye but he kept his head down, counting and banding the cash in five-hundreds. Brendan had not spoken since they had left Dundalk, and why would he, what was there to say? Here they were, crossing the border with an armoured police pursuit, the smell of the money starting to fill the car interior, the grubby handled odour of it, and Jean felt imperilled not by thieves or by police but by her own heart that had led her to this, misplaced love a contraband from the start.

The car behind would not turn on blue lights for that would identify it as police and they did not want to be known so there was little to separate it from the traffic around it save for the bulletproof glass and the heavy black frames which held the glass in place. This was a killing zone. They passed the Edenappa Road where the bodies of two policemen had been found earlier that month, one on the ground, the other in the driver's seat, the side of his head cleanly removed by a copper-jacketed round so that you could see the brain in cutaway like an anatomy plate from an old book, and the policemen following the Mercedes knew of it and would have known the men and they did not slow. The fact that you couldn't see them was worse, Jean said afterwards, these faceless men like vengeance itself pursued them.

Even with the weight of armour the Cortina kept tight to the Mercedes, and cars and lorries ahead of them saw or at least felt the onrush of the two cars and took to the hard shoulder. On this road of all border roads you didn't need to be told that a Mercedes and an armoured police car travelling at high speed feet apart was something you wanted to stay away from. As this pursuit neared the metal railway bridge at Cloghogue Brendan's face was set and impassive. Jean could see the Enterprise crossing the bridge in front of them. She wanted to tell Brendan that she was afraid but she knew he would not hear her. She looked at the speedometer as they started the long bend into the descent towards the bridge and then she looked back and although she could not see the driver of the police car through the bulletproof windscreen she knew he was feeling the weight of the car and the momentum granted the ton of armour plating and knew that it was already too late. She waited for Brendan to look at his mirror for he must have known it too, the Mercedes itself on the edge.

The police car started to slide, the body of the car tilted, weight forward, the tyres smoking, and as the Mercedes passed the apex of the bend the police car slowly turned around its own apex, crossed the opposite lane and was lost behind the smoke of its tyres.

Brendan did not even look in the mirror. It was not that men like Brendan did not look back because they wouldn't. They could not look back on the desolation of their choices. Owen had not raised his head the whole time.

The cash had come through and it was a big night in McCrink's, everybody dressed to the nines. Brendan was there with Jean, buying drinks fit to beat the band. Eamon. There was a good-looking man she thought was Eamon's associate, Mackin. A red-haired solicitor from Newry, Leo White. John Carney, a building contractor who cashed big cheques in the Bureau. In the Bureau Carney carried more mystery than most. No one had seen any of his buildings, the construction projects he spoke of, the road projects. He talked about sea armour he had constructed to protect marginal land on the north coast, fenlands drained, improvements carried out. He was weary, overburdened. All the good he had put in the world and how he wanted nothing back except what he was due. He drove a ten-year-old Mercedes with a cracked windscreen. The policeman Corrigan was there. Judge Cecil Hearty pulled up outside.

'Jesus,' Jean said. 'The judge is here. He has some neck on him, and his two cops outside watching the thieves' ball.'

Hutchie brought his wife Lena who you never saw out, she was small and pretty with charm bracelets on both wrists. Hutchie said when he was drunk that she had cancer but what kind he never said and she never seemed to sicken from it.

'The only cancer she's got is the one sitting on the bar stool beside her,' Jean said. Lorraine blessed herself. You never made jokes about cancer for next thing it would arrive uninvited at your own door, they'd cut her Auntie May open and seen it a big black thing the size of your fist and next thing they sewed her right up again, there was nothing they could do.

'Them's only old yarns,' Jean said, 'and if Lady Muck there has cancer she's looking well on it.'

Lorraine said her heart misgave her that the American Express job was bad luck but Jean told her to wise up, money was just money, either you had it or you don't. It wasn't going to talk to you or bring you luck good nor bad.

What had Jean crabbed was that Brendan was sitting with Lena. Lorraine heard her talking about cancer and Brendan saying he would give her a thousand pounds if she was sat on the same bar stool in a year's time cancer free. As if you could forestall dying by lottery.

'He never gave me no thousand pounds, nor offered it to me in a bet,' Jean said. Lorraine was afraid Jean would follow Lena into the toilets. Jean was the best in the world but she could be coarse in language and manner and Lorraine had no wish to be caught up in some drama of pulled hair and uncouth phrases.

'He hasn't given any money to her yet,' Lorraine said. 'She never done no harm to me.'

'Hark at you taking sides,' Jean said. 'At least Hutchie's not ashamed of people seeing her in the daylight.'

'Paddy takes me out.'

'To a gaff like this. He doesn't bring you to the Roadhouse on a Saturday night.'

Lorraine didn't want to be a wife in the shadows, that frail half-glimpsed thing, and when she had drunk three Bacardis she sat down beside Paddy.

'Would you bring me to Florida?'

'You wouldn't like it there.'

'How do you know?'

'You wouldn't like the heat.'

'Do you?'

'I can take it or leave it.'

You like my heat don't you though. All aboard for my heat. She didn't say it out loud though. She went to the bar and there was Corrigan edging up to her, talking out of the side of his mouth.

'You know they say that Farrell has another family.'

'I know he has another family.'

'Not that one. Another family in London.'

'Who says that?'

'People say it. He lived in London for a few years. They say he set up shop with some woman there. Had a family with her.'

'I don't believe you.'

'Only telling you. Word is she moved to Australia. With her little family.'

A woman with children, wan, abandoned. Pushing a pram through precincts, places unknown to her. All she knew of London was famous buildings and housing estates. She could see Paddy with a skinny pale girl with slum child looks. 'He has a taste for the trashy ones,' Corrigan said. She turned her back on him and his charlatan whispering.

Brendan bought bottles of Montrachet and Chablis for them all. Jean said it was wasted on them, you might as well pour it down a drain. Hutchie raised toasts to American Express and to the passport service. It was the first time American Express was mentioned that night although it was the reason they were there, the money they made, the policemen's hearts they broke. Paddy didn't like it. Mocking is catching, he said. There could be no luck with talk the like of it. Hutchie like a jester now, full drunk and mouthy. Jean was sitting in a red velvet banquette with the builder Carney and she couldn't work him out. Paddy was still sitting at the corner of the bar. He was a quiet drinker. Lorraine didn't know where he went at such times.

Lena was still sitting beside Brendan. She was telling him that the name Carlingford meant 'Carling's fjord' after some Viking. Hutchie said it was a fjord with the narrow seaway and the high mountains around it, the steep sides going down almost to the water's edge.

'It isn't a fjord,' Lorraine said, 'you only get them in Norway.'

'Hark at little Miss Brainbox,' Lena said.

'Strictly speaking,' Brendan said, 'Lorraine's right. It's only a fjord if the water inside is deeper than the water outside.'

'Miss vinegar tits doesn't look one bit impressed,' Jean said.

Lorraine tried not to smile. Paddy didn't like women who squabbled with each other. He told her it wasn't dignified, and she almost said that kicking seven policemen half to death and ending up in gaol wasn't very dignified either but she kept her beak shut. You didn't take that kind of liberty with Paddy. He wasn't that kind of man. Paddy was described in the newspapers

as a *drug baron*. The evidence for this is sparse. He was said
to have been working with named individuals, bringing drugs
through Dublin port and across the border to be distributed in
the North through paramilitary contacts and others. If that is
so, then something careful in him had started to give way.

It was the first time Jean set eyes on Speedy Fegan. Speedy
was blond and blue-eyed with cropped hair. He was wearing
an aviator jacket and had a thick gold chain around his neck.
Hutchie said they called him Speedy because he liked fast cars,
although Jean said he didn't look old enough to have a driving
licence never mind spinning around the place in flashy motors.

'I heard tell of you and Paddy to be fair to him he has a
good eye in his head, I'm Cathal Fegan but I go by the name
of Speedy, Speedy by name Speedy by nature, I'm in business
so I am the happy business I bet Paddy would like to be in the
happy business too I'll talk to him Lorraine you'll help me talk
to him won't you? I'm running a trotting race in Sunday youse
can all come I'm no rider myself but I've plenty of boys who are.'

'Slow down, son,' Bann said, 'you'll dislocate your jawbox
talking that fast.'

'I'll be alright, Mr Bann,' Speedy said. 'Can I get you a
drink, a dark rum?'

'I'll buy my own. It's hard on the ponies, the trotting,' Bann
said.

'It's cruel,' Jean said, 'them men lashing the poor horses.'

'To be fair the driver'd never touch them,' Speedy said. 'He might show them the whip now and then, that would be the height of it.'

Eamon went behind the bar and put a Philomena Begley LP on the stereo, some old-time music of broken lives. Music they all liked, music of the left behind, unvisited graves, lost dustbowl loves. They were fine with other people's regrets but were impenitent with regard to their own doings. Like the other men in the bar that night and Dominic in his on-the-run mountain house. They did not sorrow for what they had done but if they could not bend things to their will something maimed was awakened in them. Not regret but its unwholesome other.

Hutchie said that Dominic could not cross the border for fear of arrest and that was why he wasn't there, but Lorraine didn't think that Dominic was afraid of arrest. That he was out there in the hunted dark made their celebration seem paltry. Mornings she'd turn on the radio in the Peugeot for news of border raids, of ambuscades, men gunned down in front of their families, and she thought of Dominic and his mannish wife absorbed in the consequence of themselves and the place they fled to that no light entered. If there was a country song for Dominic and Mary, it would be one of blood and vendetta and loss.

Lorraine sat beside Judge Cecil Hearty. The judge's eyes were veined with drink and there was a tremor in his hand. He told her that at university Brendan had wanted to be a leader of progressive politics. He said that Brendan had wanted to go to Eastern Europe and take part in revolution against repressive governments, street protests. They were both young men driven by idealism, and that they went to screenings of political documentaries, bloody uprisings in monochrome.

The judge said that they had watched too many of these films and that in the end they seemed to be watching the same death again and again. There is a body lying on the street in front of a university, the trousers have ridden up showing the socks. A dark suit, shabby in death. The blood looks blackish, tarry. The head is turned away but there seemed to be always thick-framed spectacles on the ground, one lens starred. The two young men found it hard to see past the dead man and these dense photographed moments, minutes after a shooting. This is how Brendan had seen himself dying but it was too late for that now. The judge was drunk and said dying in this manner would have been better for Brendan and for the judge himself in the long run.

When Lorraine went outside Paddy was in the street with Hutchie. Hutchie was pressed against the mosaic front of Hughes Bookmakers. The mosaic showed a horse and jockey with the rider in bright silks bent over the horse's neck. There was foam on the horse's mouth and there were weals on its flanks. Paddy had his right hand at Hutchie's throat. Hutchie's mouth was open but no sound came forth. Paddy placed the palm of his left hand over Hutchie's good eye. Hutchie's chest was rising and falling. Paddy's hand making a mask.

'Easy,' Paddy said. 'Easy.' As if it was the horse he was talking to. As if he addressed a spooked beast that would shy and buck and needed to be gentled.

'You're mouthing too much about American Express,' Paddy said. 'You need to keep the beak shut or I'll fucking blind you.'

'I'll never mention it again.' Hutchie said. 'I swear.'

'You can't lower yourself to Hutchie's level,' Lorraine said on the way home.

'I never hurt him,' Paddy said.

'He looked scared out of his wits.'

'He needs to learn not to be mouthing off in bars. I showed him.' Showing him what it was like to be eyeless. Showing him what eternal lightlessness would mean. Lorraine remembered the mosaic, the horse lathered, eyes wide, straining for the line.

'I never hurt him, but I showed him the whip,' Paddy said.

Ten

There was a lot of easy money on the border. Too much easy money by Paddy's reckoning, as if he considered his own money hard-earned. A family fuel smugglers called Devine bought a Hotel just south of Dundalk. The Hotel was known for its dance hall and lavish border weddings but things changed when it was sold. They brought sand from the beach at Giles Quay in lorries and spread it on the sprung wooden floor of the function room and had a grand opening party with beach umbrellas and waitresses in bikinis serving cocktails. They invited hundreds of people and called it a Beach Party. Jean pretended she didn't want to go. She said she didn't want to be leered at and groped by flash bastards but she was straight into Snaubs for an outfit when Brendan said they were invited. The outfit was all shoulderpads and tits, Hutchie said. Lorraine would not have used vulgar words in such a manner, but Paddy just laughed and said each to their own.

Lorraine liked to wear a dress low-cut at the back and then when they were going out to ask Paddy to zip her into it. She thought her back was one of her best features and she knew it would look good with the strap of a new bra across it and her hair arranged with tendrils falling down. She imagined it was a wife's back, the little bones, the vertebrae, pale knuckles to be counted by a man's fingers. She bent her head forward so that he could see the nape of her neck and the downy hairs on it. Standing like that and feeling his hands on the zip she felt owned. She wanted to ask him if he had ever zipped up the English girl's dress.

Lorraine told Paddy it was important to mix with the right people but that wasn't the way Paddy did things. Business was above all to be guarded, cryptic, conducted in asides and subtle tells. He knew that the Devines were facing serious charges relating to fuel smuggling and he didn't want to be associated with it which Jean said was a bit rich coming from Paddy.

Lorraine talked Paddy round but when it came to it Lorraine didn't know if she wanted to go. There was talk of men and women at each other right in front of your eyes and car keys put in bowls. The idea of drunkenness and bedrooms being booked by the hour made her feel strange, there was an end of days feel to it. Bann said that he wouldn't go to a place where men and women gave themselves up to debauch and fornication.

'You'd go if they were giving out rum for free,' Hutchie said. 'If the old Captain Morgan's was on tap wild horses wouldn't drag you away.' Bann said that he conceded the point and even Nora smiled.

Lorraine bought a blouse with a high neckline and a pleated skirt which went to below the knee. She had her hair done in a bob and kept the make-up to a minimum, did everything she could to say hands off. As if, Jean said, anybody with any sense was going to risk getting fresh with Paddy's woman. Lorraine wanted to say that she wasn't doing it for anyone bar herself but she could see that Paddy liked it when she got into the car that night, smoothing her skirt as she sat down and keeping her knees together and her back very straight. He put his hand on her knee but she lifted it off again prim as you like.

The foyer of the hotel was all fake palm trees and there were girls wearing palm skirts with flowers in their hair holding trays of drinks, the palm skirts already tattered and the flowers wilted in the heat. The male guests were wearing Hawaiian shirts and shorts or floral skirts and some of the women were wearing bikini tops which made Lorraine feel stupid and overdressed but Paddy said he liked her respectable and she said to herself do you now?

'They'll be falling out of them tops when they've a few drinks in them,' he said, and Jean whispered in her ear where did Mr fucking Manners come from? There was a trail of damp sand on the foyer carpet which had been carried from the ballroom. Lorryloads of sand had been left under the stage. Lorraine smelt salt and half-rotted kelp, marine smells that underlay the perfume and aftershave and cigarette smoke, the dance floor full and the men looking red-faced and leering already.

'You're not getting me out there,' Lorraine said, 'they can keep their hands to themselves.'

'You're like a chicken waiting to be plucked, sweetheart,' Jean said.

'And you aren't?'

'I look like shite,' Jean said.

'You look great,' Lorraine said, though Jean did look rough. Brendan had been drinking hard that week. He would be drunk when he came to bed and that was when he craved a dissolution from her that was greater than his own, the clotted mascara, the chipped nail varnish, the slip showing under the hem of her skirt, standing in a hotel room, half dressed, demoralized. Jean did not understand these unwholesome cravings, their tending deathward, but she knew how to cater to them.

'Kind of you, I'm sure,' Jean said, 'but the state I'm in no other man would look near me. I couldn't get a dog to bark at me. What do men want anyway?'

'What're you two looking so miserable for?' Eamon was

wearing a Hawaiian shirt and shorts and holding a drink with an umbrella in it. 'Aloha!'

'Aloha my hole,' Jean said.

'There's the bosses now,' Eamon said.

'Bosses of what?'

'The whole show. Devine and the missus.'

Devine dark and stocky, the same height as Paddy, wearing a brown suit and slip-ons, shirt collar open, tie pulled loose at the neck. Newspapers called him an oil baron, smuggling charges had been brought on the northern side of the border, an extradition request was being prepared. You'd swear him some swart Camorra glad-handing party guests, taking a roll of cash from his trouser pocket and putting it behind the bar, free drinks until it runs out, he's that kind of man, a smile for all, Devine will buy you out from under yourself. That's Devine but the wise money looks at the wife Faye Devine, see her in flat-soled pumps and white linen trouser suit. She's got a gold charm bracelet, and heavy gold earrings, a deepwater tan with liver spots on her neck and arms. She wears glasses on a chain around her neck. The eyes are shrewd, amused and always watching and there is something of death in them.

'I hear tell she's the real boss, she runs the show and he does the donkey work.'

'There's a pair of them in it,' Eamon said. Jean started to laugh.

'What the fuck are you laughing at?' Hutchie said. Jean pointed.

'Look who's coming in the glad rags. Fucking Bann.'

'It's the sailor boy, must have the Captain Morgan's on tap after all,' Lorraine said, but she was glad to see Bann.

Bann was wearing a navy blue blazer with gold buttons and grey slacks, a tie with anchors on it, his hair brylcreemed back, a merchant seaman's badge in his lapel.

'Thought there was too much sin and fornication for you,' Jean said.

'I'll turn the eyes away when there's fornication going on,' Bann said. 'Shall we?'

An aged and drink-shook debonair, he took Lorraine by the arm, and walked her onto the dance floor. Hutchie offered his arm to Jean but she told him to go fuck himself. The band were playing Elvis, the Tennessee Waltz, and Bann led Lorraine, two-stepping across the sprung dance floor with one hand on her hip and the other holding her right arm high following Bann's lead and she wished she was wearing a skirt that flowed, something diaphonous that swept, that if she shut her eyes she could float for ever and be enraptured.

'Fred and Ginger,' Jean said.

'More like brandy and ginger,' Hutchie said. But Bann could dance and none of them had known it.

*

Blue Hawaii was running on a projector at the side of the dance hall, the film projected onto the east wall, Elvis in a navy cap singing 'Moonlight Swim' in an open-top sedan with four girls. Cigarette smoke wreathing through the projector beam the way it used to in the Adelphi, Lorraine a teenager in the napped velvet seats at the back, all else felt forlorn and long ago, Elvis with flowers around his neck singing to Doris Day, paper lanterns over their heads in the garlanded night. *I can't help falling in love with you.*

Corrigan came over to their banquette and pulled up a gilded ballroom chair. Hutchie and Paddy nodded to him. Lorraine could feel his eyes on her. Before she had Paddy she would have met his look brazen as you like but now she felt part of a bogey enterprise with every word and look a jeopardy.

'We're all dressed up tonight girls, aren't we? A right little bunch of gangsters' molls indeed. Fell into a right den of thieves, didn't you?'

'The detective thinks you've took up with bad company, Lorraine,' Hutchie said.

'None worse than himself,' Jean said in a low voice.

'Are you a sporting man, Hutchie?' Corrigan said so that Lorraine and Jean couldn't hear him. 'For if you are I'm giving you odds here and now that girl won't see thirty.'

'What makes you think that?' Hutchie said. Corrigan shook his head.

'If somebody said that about me I'd take it as a threat,' Hutchie said.

'Take it whatever way you want,' Corrigan said.

Brendan was sitting at a table at the back of the room with the woman Faye Devine. They had their heads together and they were laughing like old friends and Jean saw the woman place her hand on Brendan's knee and leave it there. She was older than Jean and maybe even older than Brendan but there was an unwholesome glamour to her that men liked and maybe Brendan as well for he had a taste for the defiled she well knew.

Faye got up first and Jean wished her gone but Brendan stood up as well and they went out of the ballroom together.

'I'm going after him,' Jean said.

'Stay here,' Lorraine said.

'I've followed better men into worse places.' Jean got up. 'Nobody's pulling no wool over my eyes.'

'For fuck's sake,' Lorraine said.

This was a wing of the hotel which had not been re-opened and it was blowsy and disused. There were missing banisters on the stairs, the carpets faded and worn to the nap. Brendan and Faye stepped left at the top of the stairs. Jean waited until they had turned the corner and then she followed them. The corridor had windows on one side, the window glass cracked

and starred, damp-stained curtains suspended from their archi-
traves. A bedroom door hung half off its hinges. She could see
an unmade bed in the room, tossed nylon sheets heir to old
assignations, and she shivered as if she had taken part although
she had not, not at this hotel, not in those sheets. At the end of
the corridor a service door was propped open with a half-block,
one turn within it leading to a boiler room, the furnace cold and
silent, and the other leading to a glassed-in office, the kind of
place where takings were counted, a tally place. She was in the
shadow and was hidden from Brendan and Faye and she could
not hear what they were saying. They had lists in front of them.
Faye was reading out names and Brendan was taking notes. To
plot came naturally to Faye and Brendan. It came naturally to
all of them. Faye turned to the iron safe behind her and took
out two banded bundles of notes and called out a name and
Jean inched forward. There was an anteroom to the side of the
office and she could see figures through the bevelled glass. One
of them stood and entered the office, a gaunt tall man she didn't
recognize. Faye handed him the two bundles of cash and he left.

Jean knew that she should not be there and wasn't surprised
when a man's hands took hold of her forearms. Hutchie. She
recognized his smell, the gaolhouse odour that he could not
conceal under the aftershave he used. There was a rankness of
incarcerate maleness and dawn slop-outs that some men could
not shed after they had left prison.

'What are you doing here, Jeanie?' Hutchie said.

'Don't call me that.'

'What?'

'Jeanie.'

'Why would I not call you Jeanie?'

Hutchie loosened his grip on her arms but she did not turn around. She didn't want to look at that fake eye, the lewd tilt of it.

'What did you think? That he was up here with some woman?'

'No.' She wanted to tell him that she didn't know what she might find in the unlit corridors of the hotel unless it was to confirm that Brendan was a man and faithless like all others.

'He'll never leave his wife, you know that?' But Jean didn't want Brendan to leave his wife. She believed that subterfuge was what she had with Brendan and that they would be nothing without it.

'She doesn't want Brendan to leave his wife.' Hutchie did not look round when he heard Lorraine but he let go of Jean's arms.

'A right pair of adulterers we have here, isn't that right?'

'Don't call us that.' Lorraine didn't like the word. Thou shalt not commit. The words sin-etched in her mind.

'I'll call you whatever I like when you're sneaking around spying on people.'

'Leave us alone, you one-eyed bastard,' Jean said.

'I might only have the one eye,' Hutchie said, 'but it sees

fucking everything. The two of youse in this hotel and you can't tell what's going on right in front of them baby blues of yours.'

'Well maybe you'd tell us, Mr Smarty.' Lorraine didn't care but she didn't want to be reminded about Paddy's wife. She could also tell that Jean wanted her to change the conversation, that Jean could content herself with another woman's leavings but she didn't want to be reminded of it by a one-eyed fucker standing behind her in the basement.

'Beach party,' Hutchie said. 'You think they put this whole show on for nothing? Do the Devines look like the kind of people who throw money away?'

Down below them Lorraine could then see Brendan and Faye bent over their list and did ask herself what they were doing there, shadowed, whispering and crabbed in the dark. What were any of them doing there?

Later Lorraine wondered if it wasn't Corrigan after all but the Beach Party had given Paddy the idea of not just holidaying in Florida but of living there. That somewhere among the tilted beach umbrellas and fake palm trees and damp sand in the ballroom he had found that there was a grace of living long denied him, warm gulf winds blowing from the south. The Everglades, Key Largo. There were salt flats, long vistas out to a flat metallic sea with the burnish of the sun on it. She saw Paddy walking on sand spits, ankle-deep in warm salt water. She saw him old, sun-blotched in a golf buggy, hipped and shuffling. She would not have that for him. She would not have him grow old in the blinding Florida light.

Bann said that the bad luck started when Speedy came on the scene but the truth was that they were their own bad luck. They would never make virtuous dead. The Bureau was busy. Some days there were queues down the street and they stood up to their knees in uncounted cash. Speedy was decades younger than Brendan but that didn't seem to matter.

'He's two things that Brendan likes. He's got a lot of cash that he needs to get rid of. And he's fond of a bet.'

Speedy was as good as his word in one thing and he introduced them to sulky racing. A Saturday or Sunday morning was chosen when the dual carriageway running between Warrenpoint port and Newry was quiet. They'd close the roadway off by driving six cars abreast behind the racing sulkies. The police didn't approach them. There was talk that they were paid off or that Brendan had spoken to them but it was more likely that they knew it would take a major police operation to take on the sulky followers and the wildness that engulfed them when the racing began. It was better to stand aside.

Paddy drove the Bureau people to the race in a Hiace with Brendan in the passenger seat and the rest of the Bureau crew standing on the flatbed behind the cab. Bann had a forty glass bottle of Captain Morgan's and he stood without holding on to the sides like the merchant seaman he had once been and he acknowledged onlookers. Speedy pulled alongside in the Mitsubishi to salute him and Bann returned the gesture, touching the rum bottle to his temple like some depraved commander.

After Paddy's death the newspapers reported that he was involved with Speedy in the drug trade but they did not produce any evidence.

The sulkies were light jigs dorsal hitched and pulled by a single horse with the boy jockeys sitting on the front of the slender frame just behind the horse. Large amounts were bet on these races, the horses high-stepping, the boys carrying long whips perched, the road closed because they had ordained it so, men in vans and jeeps following the jigs at speed sitting in the windows or standing on jeep beds, driving oncoming traffic onto the pavements and verges, bare-chested men streaming their shirts behind them in closed fists like tattered regalia, the bannered outlawry of the afternoon.

After the sulky race Speedy and others went to the Hermitage bar on Canal Street just around the corner from Brendan's old office in Catherine Street. Speedy drove the Mitsubishi. That week he'd walked into Keogh Cars showroom and put the price of the car down on the counter in twenty-pound notes.

'Paid the same for the pony that won, the piebald Standard-bred,' he said. 'Brought her from Australia. Sulkies is legal there.'

'No good when it's legal,' Hutchie said.

'You have a point there, Hutchie,' Speedy said. 'You have a definite point.'

'Cowboys,' Bann said. 'Youse are all fucking cowboys.'

Eleven

Colm McKevitt was asleep at his sister's house when two men wearing combat jackets and balaclavas kicked down the front door and took him out of bed. They put him into a van and drove past his mother's house to Jones Road where they took him out of the van and shot him in the face. His mother was standing at the kitchen sink looking out. She couldn't get a grip on what was going on. To imagine him stood in his underwear on the wintery roadside where a mother's tears could not save him. She strained to see him through the kitchen window but could not make him out, the image of her son through the rain and condensation forever sleety, marred. She knew he wasn't a good boy but he was her boy.

An IRA statement said that McKevitt had been an informer. Police said that he was known as a petty criminal but the IRA statement said that he had been involved in organized crime and that he had been given a free hand in return for intelligence. That may or may not have been so but it was not the reason he was killed. In this border country at this time you did not misstep or mistake your place. Following the removal of his body from the scene, straw was laid on the roadway to conceal and absorb McKevitt's blood, the gold and the crimson on the tarmac.

The border was said to be unpoliced but it was not without law. When Eamon walked into the Bureau to say that McKevitt was dead it did not seem to be news to anyone there and the only comment made was from Hutchie who put down his newspaper for a moment and said, 'McKevitt would have best stuck to robbing sweetie shops,' and went back to his reading.

Eamon told Lorraine afterwards that McKevitt's father was Brendan's cousin. In this land of vendetta sometimes blood counted for everything and sometimes it counted for nothing and you didn't know until it was too late.

Twelve

Owen was waiting in the Bureau to take the Enterprise mainline to Dublin. He was going back to college. It was Sunday evening and things were quiet. Brendan was reading the newspaper and smoking. Hutchie was on his stool in the corner. He was always hard to read. His face had a mutilated quality not just due to his artificial eye. He didn't like Owen. There was a slouchy thing about the young man. And a hidden thing, maybe he thought he was better than everyone else, Hutchie didn't know but he didn't like him. Passing through a checkpoint once he had told the policeman that the driver of the car behind him was drunk, which wasn't true. Owen had been pulled out of the car and breathalyzed. Hutchie had treated it as a joke but it wasn't and nobody told Brendan about it.

The front wall of the office was made of bulletproof sheet

steel covered with wood-effect beauty board. The teller's window was made of quarter-inch laminate perspex. Owen saw a car pull up outside and bent down to see the driver, the low sun made the abraded surface of the glass hard to see through. Paddy got out of a burgundy BMW 7 Series. He changed £5,000 sterling in used twenty pound notes. He placed the notes carefully in the attaché case. He always opened the case towards him so you couldn't see what was in it.

'I'm for Dublin, I'll leave the BMW here and take another car,' he said. That was it. You didn't ask anyone any of their business unless they came straight out with it. You were required to intuit things, there was a world of the withheld. Meanings shifted. They worked in gestures, card-player tells. The world was full of plants, informers, dark betrayal. If you said the wrong thing to the wrong person your words could start to follow you around. You could be hunted back through your own meaning. That's how people ended up shot. That's how you were found at the side of a border road with marks of interrogation on your body.

Paddy got up to leave and Brendan followed him out to the car. When he came back Brendan nodded at Owen.

'Paddy's going to take you to Dublin.' Owen thought Hutchie was smiling, something animate in his ruined features, his gaolhouse pallor. Life was full of bleak jokes and you never knew what turn events were going to take. You could be tripped up at any minute. Owen trying to read his father's look. He knew he was being given something here but couldn't see the meaning of it, something between fathers and sons made legacy in the moment.

Paddy turned off the main road just before the military checkpoint. They'd cross the border on one of the unmapped back roads. Everyone did it to avoid the checkpoints and road spikes, the sandbagged enclosures, the radio static and staccato military chatter, Oscar, Tango, Bravo. Nobody was fooled any more. To go down the main road through the military checkpoints was to adhere to convention. To travel down the back roads was to go rogue in your own country, you started to feel like an infiltrator, deeply networked. The terms of engagement on the back roads were clear to everyone, everyone was careful. The troops dropped in by helicopter and set up temporary checkpoints. There were foxgloves and dog roses in the ditches. Owen didn't remember what they talked about on the first few miles but he remembered that the car wasn't one of Paddy's top range models, one of the Mercedes, or BMW 7 series. It was an Escort, a little shabby, a little dinged, the interior grimed, dirt ingrained in the dash plastic, hard miles and too many of them on the clock. You were meant to see a man on the way home from a job, a tiler, a plasterer, a mechanic. Everything about the car indicated a life of hardwon gains, life in increments. Paddy going undercover in the hard-won, the tax disc expired, more small life concerns than you can take with you.

They were stopped a mile north of the border. Two soldiers in the middle of the road, Royal Greenjackets, their faces blacked, mud on their boots, they'd been dropped in by Lynx or Puma, defiling from the helicopter before it touched the ground. There was a soldier in the ditch, camouflage netting pulled over a general-purpose machine gun. You were neither anonymous or identified. You had to prove yourself in ways unknown. The soldier asked for ID and Paddy took a driving licence from the sun visor and handed it over. Paddy had a way of gathering in on himself, you felt the containment, the shielding, gathering the ordinary around him so that no one could see the danger in him. The soldier stood away from the car and read the licence details into the radio.

These border roads were illicit. Crossings had been cratered, bridges blown up or closed by concrete and metal traps. Once you used them your guilt was assumed until you proved otherwise. Shopping trips became illicit, family visits. You weren't supposed to be here, some power did not wish it, a power that was not quite explained by the subterfuge that seemed implicit to the landscape, a stirring in the whitethorn ditches and whins and fieldstone divisions. There were no signposts. You had to know where you were going and the destinations were not solely geographic. The almanac of this place was ornamented with booby-trapped bodies in black bin-bags, hunched and monkish on undrained verges. The soldier handed the driving licence back to Paddy and told him to open the boot, Paddy got out and left the licence on the driver's seat. Owen picked it up and looked at it. The photograph was Paddy, photobooth monochrome, looking sickly, caught in some kind of corpse light.

They were stopped twice more by police and by customs. Paddy used another driving licence and a passport for identification. The photographs were all from the same batch but the names were different. Owen said nothing and Paddy started to relax and talk to him. Some kind of forger's code established between them, some low-key untested bond. They took the back road through Slane into Dublin, long, straight, tree-lined. Owen tried to remember afterwards what they talked about but he could only recall their conversation as they passed the Four Courts on Aston Quay close to the city centre. Paddy joked that in a few years' time he would be in the dock as the defendant and Owen wearing a barrister's wig would be standing up to question him as the prosecutor. And that shortly after Paddy dropped him off in College Green in the centre of the town, Owen thought he would see Paddy alive again but he did not.

Thirteen

Paddy and Lorraine flew from Aldergrove to Liverpool. Paddy on what he called a business trip. A gusty October evening with night come early and the leafless trees asway on the airport road so that the wings of the plane flexed as it took off. Lorraine leaned her arm against his shoulder and held on tight to his bicep, feeling it move as he turned the pages of the inflight magazine, they did not feel fear these men, she thought, who should be in terror in a plane blown about in the constellate dark.

Looking down from the window of the 737 as it banked. The lights of Liverpool Airport and the Mersey below, flying over the muddy inlets and sandbanks, drizzle beading on the window.

He brought her to the Adelphi Hotel in Liverpool. Paddy had bought luggage in Belfast, hand baggage in leatherette and a

Louis Vuitton case with brass locks. She waited for him to say something about how many shoes she had brought but he did not. She emptied the cases and hung shirts and blouses in the wardrobes and everything folded in drawers. Paddy had brought a holdall of cash which he put at the back of the wardrobe. He said that she did not have to empty everything out of the cases but this room was hers, and she hung lace garments in the closets, her things perfumed, her things silken, what was all of the finest, what was all of the sheerest. She wanted him to know what she had bought for him.

She stood in front of Paddy and started to undo his tie and then his shirt. She could see her own eyes in the mirror behind him and there was something lustful and strange in them, deceits she did not recognize and had yet to practise. She looked like a glittery-eyed woman from a film. Another woman's husband. She lay back on the bed her skirt riding up her thighs and looked up at him. She wanted to reach into him for the long held part, to have what she could purloin from the wife trove. She put her fingers against the still unhealed cut on his eyebrow and thought if he could once be peeled open, the skin rolled back from there, he would be hers in blood and bone.

They drove in morning light through the northern industrial zones, the flats and scrublands between motorways. Gas flare from the refinery by the river and a taste of heavy metals in the mouth. Passing shut-down industrial plants, security company logos on rusted chain link fences, asbestos roofing holed and broken and hanging, glimpses of steel fabricated interiors, broken cranes, unfired furnaces. Car auctions were held on old factory hardstandings on the margins of the industrial zone, used vehicles, lined off into the distance, Z regs, Korean imports, Transit and Hiace vans.

Lorraine wanted to ask Paddy how he knew where he was going and how often he had been here, but there were times you knew you couldn't talk to him, break into his thoughts, how things might play out in arcs of delicate crookery. He could say cruel things if you intruded on his thinking.

A taxi left them at a dented sheet metal gate. Paddy said to wait beside the prefab at the entrance. He walked away from her into the rows of cars with his briefcase. It was cold at the gate and men looked at her as they drove past. Some of them made gestures though she was well fit for men and their crude words and besides it gave her satisfaction to think of what might happen if Paddy had seen them. But her feet were cold and she had not dressed to stand for hours on end. She was wearing kitten heels with fine tights and a bronze gilet with a linen jacket that the wind blowing across the flatlands from the sea cut through. When a Jaguar XJ6 came out of the gates she was fit to be tied, but the door of the car swung open, Paddy at the wheel. All aboard, he said. He turned onto the motorway sliproad and joined the M6 towards Liverpool and the ferry back to Belfast, driving under powerlines, the pylons on the flatland refinery, gas flare on the horizon as if the road they were on led through nameless tracts to the end of the world.

After the trip to the Midlands Lorraine started to buy things from mail order catalogues. She bought stockings and suspenders. Lacy stuff. Peephole things. Although she did not like looking at the illustrations, girls in boots and whips. There were leathers and vinyls, black and red. She did not think when she was kissing boys in the dunes that it would all become so involved. She could wear the clothes, the stiletto boots and corsets but the elaborations that came with them weren't available to her. She wanted to be lurid and tragic, not standing over a man with a whip not knowing what to do with it.

'That's the trouble,' Jean said, 'you have to be everything.' Men like Brendan and Paddy were sentimental, Jean said, for all they were at you all the time they liked to buy their women the same presents they bought their mothers.

'It's all swank one minute and their sainted mother the next,' Jean said.

'I hope he doesn't do to his mother what he does to me,' Lorraine said.

'Oh dear sweet Jesus, there's dirty talk and then there's just plain filth,' Jean said. But it was true. On Lorraine's birthday Paddy bought her large pink padded cards with teddy bears on the front and a rhyme inside. On Valentine's Day he bought her a dozen roses and jewellery with heart designs. He liked her to dress for bed in pastel shades, shortie nightdresses with fur trim on the hem, little baby girl things worn with white lace stockings. When she first stood in front of him in the bedroom in her flat wearing a black basque and heels she thought that he was going to hit her.

Fourteen

'Eamon's dead.'

'Oh dear Jesus.'

'Cullyhanna. Him and Mackin found shot dead in the car. Locked in the boot and the car left by the side of the road.'

'Jesus, oh fucking Jesus,' Jean said.

Paddy walked through the door and just came out with the dire news, flat and unadorned. Brendan looked off into the distance. Eamon being killed was something that happened and now it had to be thought through, how it affected their interests, how close it came to them, did others have to be talked to, were there people who had to be reassured? There were hierarchies to be considered. Who among the trigger happy had to be assuaged? Brendan would need a drink, time to think and set some boundaries about the event. There was an eagerness in the room to get out and about. They had heard the fact but they needed the fragments, the half-asides, the ornamented and unseemly lore of dying along the border. You had to hear how Eamon and Mackin's deaths were spoken of, you had to listen to how it was told. Had anyone seen it coming? Who had last been in their company? Had they brought it on themselves? Didn't everybody bring it on themselves? Paddy and Brendan occupying the space in the office but no mistaking the distress settling in the room, the feeling of end times, Bann saying the wages of sin is death, over and over again.

'This could be very close to home,' Hutchie said, and Paddy looked at him thoughtfully as though the space Hutchie sat in could be better occupied, or not occupied at all. 'Well, it could be,' Hutchie said.

They said that Eamon and Mackin's bodies had been found in the boot of Eamon's car. That their hands were bound behind their backs. That they had been there for days. That they had both been shot in the forehead and there were powder burns on Eamon's skin although how could this be told if his body had been there for days and subject to dissolution, unmapping itself from within? They said that they had fallen out with someone over a lorryload of smuggled dry goods. They said that there had been a falling-out over stolen Post Office money orders. A large amount of money orders had passed through the Bureau a few weeks beforehand but Brendan didn't mention them and no one took it upon themselves to bring it up. The talk was that money had been owed to the McGlincheys and that Mary had lured the two men to the car park behind the Imperial Hotel and that Dominic had shot them both there, then the bodies were put into the boot of Eamon's car and driven to Cullyhanna.

There had been no public disagreement. There had been no summons to a meeting to sort things out, a parlay off the beaten track deep into some ambush run, you had to trust the person you were meeting. But there was already bad blood between Eamon McMahon and McGlinchey. Two years before Dominic had narrowly escaped being killed by police in a checkpoint set-up. He blamed a man called Eric Dale who was married to Eamon's sister. That May a group of armed and masked men led by McGlinchey came to Dale's door. The elders were in flower. There were dog roses in the ditches and field walls.

The last time Dale's wife saw her husband alive he was lying on the ground surrounded by six armed men. Two days later his body wrapped in plastic was left on the border between Newry and Dundalk. There were signs that he had been tortured.

Hutchie had another version of the killing. 'Dale was fucking Mary McGlinchey when Dominic was in the prison. He was some brave boy to be riding McGlinchey's wife. Moth to a flame I reckon. I hope she was worth it.'

'Them's just rumours,' Bann said, 'you've no call repeating

them.' But Lorraine thought of Mary with a lover like a haunting. Where would you go to have illicit sex with Mary McGlinchey, what place would be adequate to it, what backstreet bedroom or lonely car park, what place of lonesome coupling? Where would you hide yourself afterwards, marked with the sweetness and peril of it?

The rumours wouldn't go away. It was said that Mary continued the relationship with Mackin while Dominic was in prison, that they were lost in a flare in the dark affair where the body burns like a flame. This seems unlikely. It would have taken a brave man to cheat on McGlinchey but such foolhardiness becomes some men. It falls to them to covet what belongs to another.

'They think Dominic killed Eamon,' Lorraine told Paddy. 'Did he?'

'Doesn't matter what he did or didn't do. It's what they think that counts.'

'Who's they, Paddy? When you talk about they, who do you mean?'

'That doesn't matter either. There's always someone out there.'

'I thought everybody was scared of Dominic?'

'Everybody is.'

'You never talk about it.'

'What's there to know? What's there to tell?'

Paddy was right. You either tell all of it or you tell none of it. And there's no way to tell all of it.

Lorraine remembered the feel of Eamon's hands around her waist when he lifted her to see the television in the Lorne and how he had made her suddenly weightless, able to see to the world from a height, adrift from all about. That night she kept looking at the door for Eamon, that he would enter, somehow risen, his eyes starlit, journeyed. He would lift her high above everything her life had become and his grip around her waist would not slacken.

Eamon. It wasn't that he had it coming, just that it was coming.

You do not think of the border as a place. It isn't a map location. There are no coordinates. It is razor wire on forest margins. It is a beach where the drowned are washed up. It is a desert where men and women die of thirst in the white dust. It is guard posts spaced at regular intervals with minefields between. It is fenced. It is mined. It is the eyes of night creatures caught in the beam of a spotlight. It is a sentry lighting a cigarette. It is a dog barking in the night.

Fifteen

In the car on Water Street, November lock-up, waiting for Brendan to come out of the Bureau, you're always alert, there's always a chancer with a handgun or a sawn-off ready to rob the place and leave you lying in your heart's blood on wet tarmac. Lorraine in the back seat, Hutchie driving. They were to cross the border and meet Paddy in the Imperial when it came on the car radio about Dominic. A police patrol had stumbled across a safe house and there had been a siege and a shoot-out which ended with Dominic arrested. There had been bullet-riddled cars, all the desperado hours in a lonely farmhouse somewhere in the deep country. No one had been killed but Dominic had emptied seven magazines of hollow point 303 bullets at armed detectives, wounding one of them. The *Clare Echo* described it as a western style shoot out. Dominic and Mary had been on the run for eighteen months. They had robbed a bank in Foynes and had been stopped twice at checkpoints, both times overwhelming and disarming policemen, taking their arms and uniforms. It was claimed that Dominic had to persuade Mary not to kill the policemen. Photographs from the scene showed a bullet-riddled police Ford Cortina in the foreground, the high calibre automatic bullets having passed through the car.

'McGlinchey.' Hutchie turned the radio off. 'Some boy. Some operator.'

'Was he hurt?'

'Not McGlinchey. He'll not go down easy. You know how many people he's killed?'

'No. Paddy doesn't talk about them things.'

'Maybe he should. Dominic and Mary. Wherever them two go dying goes with them. You ever hear of Sparky Barkley?'

'Don't be telling Lorraine the like of that, don't you be listening to him, daughter,' Bann said.

'You may as well tell me now,' Lorraine said.

'So him and Mary walk in on Sparky. Sparky's watching TV. They shoot him in the back of the head.'

'That's enough of that, Hutchie,' Bann said.

'Lorraine says to tell her so I'm telling her. Anyway they reckon dead Sparky's too heavy to carry out to the car without anyone noticing so they takes him into the bathroom and drain the blood out of his veins to lighten the load.'

'Why do you have to go and tell her things like that, Hutchie? Never you mind him and his yarns,' Bann said.

'It's alright.' Lorraine remembering the drained corpses of the geese in the moonlight and the mink, the little blood-drinkers watchful in the field wall.

In late May Dominic was arrested and charged for the murder of a seventy-five-year-old widow, Hester McMullen, who had been killed when McGlinchey had riddled her house in an attempt to kill members of her family.

The main road across the border from Newry to Dundalk broadens just before you reach the border, going from two lanes to seven or eight lanes wide. You feel exposed in the expanse of tarmac, the paved-over site of the customs station which was bombed seven times before being destroyed. The destroyed building had an open European feel to it, the walls of maple planks with continuous windows, you thought of light-filled interiors, a spirit of cooperation, progress being made towards agreed aims. The roof was a wing-like structure, upswept at either side, and extended thirty feet over each roadway, modernist, sheltering. The bombers came back seven times because each time, the blast blew through the girdered shell carrying away the glass panels, leaving the structure intact.

The roadway is still raised where the baseplate lies under the tarmac. Armoured Land Rovers waited for Dominic on the site of the customs post. A southern paddy wagon escorted by Special Branch in Cortinas conveyed Dominic to the handover point. 'No show without Punch,' Hutchie said when the evening news came on in McCrink's and they saw Corrigan holding Dominic by the arm. Dominic wearing a V-neck jumper and shirt and light-coloured slacks. He isn't handcuffed, Corrigan holding his left wrist lightly. Corrigan is wearing a white linen jacket and dark tie with matching handkerchief in the breast pocket, the suit looking slightly dingy but that might just be the light, some police crime scene glare

'The shape of Corrigan,' Hutchie said. 'He's not at a fucking cocktail bar.'

'Dolled-up for the cameras.'

In the next sequence Dominic has been handed over to two northern policemen. The RUC men look purposeful compared to Corrigan. They're wearing weatherproof tunics and flak jackets and they've lowered their heads so that their peaked caps hide their faces from the cameras. Dominic looks taller than everyone else, honed by long days and nights on the run, by hunting and by killing. He looks elevated and alert. The policemen either side of him are holding his arms which are away from his body, his hands palm-up facing the camera, seen in that moment as a Christ figure from a medieval panel.

Sixteen

Sunday nights were Imperial nights which meant that Paddy was finished with the wife until the following Friday night, Jean said, and Lorraine told her to shut up it was hard enough to sit out the weekend on your own. Paddy and Lorraine at the bar like people meeting for the first time. It was the same every week. There were wounded looks, long silences, everything tentative and hanging in the air. Lorraine thinking that she would not be put aside or have her love measured out in lonesome days. At closing time Paddy would go out to reception and pay for a room in cash and get two keys and leave one on the bar in front of her and she would follow him upstairs.

Paddy was staring into the mirror behind the bar. Lorraine was speaking but she could tell he wasn't listening. He had that far-off look on his face which came when he was thinking about business and those were the times when she was frightened that she did not know him at all. 'I was talking to you,' she said. A man in a tweed sports jacket pushed in between them.

'I'm talking to him now if you don't mind, miss.' She saw Paddy's hand tighten on his glass. The barman moved to the far end of the bar.

'Don't be a stupid cunt Farrell,' the man said. His elbow was pressed into Lorraine's side, pinning her against the bar. She didn't look around but she could see him in the mirror, his face the way you'd imagine a plainclothes policeman's face to be, weighed down with consequence, all he's seen and heard visible on it, disappointed in you before you'd even met. Not Corrigan's fretful mug.

'Come on to fuck, Farrell, get up or I'll get you up.' Lorraine didn't think Paddy would put up with being spoken to like that but he stood keeping his head down, his eyes fixed on the floor at his feet. You could feel it in the air. There would be no respect between police officer and criminal like there was in the films, wary nods on the courthouse steps. *After all, we're both in this together.* No one was in this together.

The man took Lorraine's gold lamé bag off her bar stool and upended it onto the bar. 'Let's see if you're up to anything.' Lorraine was the kind of girl who kept her bag ordered, everything in its place, and it struck at her heart to see everything she was spilled and hapless, her keys and tissues and emery boards, her sanitary products and a scapular to Blessed Oliver Plunkett and everything else a girl carried to make her way in the world. The policeman took a packet of Durex from the handbag contents and held it up.

'What lucky gent are these for?' Lorraine looked down at the bar mortified. 'Good to see people being careful. You can't be careful enough as our Paddy well knows.'

'Leave her be, Dixon,' Paddy said.

'It's not me has to leave her be.'

'Lorraine, call Brendan and you know who else,' Paddy said.

'You'll have to wait for Corrigan if that's who you're talking about,' the policeman said. 'He's golfing in Spain. Though how he can afford to golf in Spain on a police salary is beyond me. Do you know, Lorraine? Maybe you'd know a bit about selling yourself to the highest bidder?'

Lorraine seeing her face in the mirror. Hair bobbed to the shoulders, blonde highlights, blue eyes, a harmed look. Something edgy and hurt about her, someone that might lash out with mean words. Dixon took Paddy out of the bar. Lorraine tried to gather her effects from the countertop. Her foundation had spilled, there was powder everywhere. 'If he'd stripped the clothes off my back and left me stood there bare to the world it would have been less embarrassing,' she told Jean.

'Well you won't have much use for the Durex for a good

while now. Could be out of date by the time they let Paddy go from what I hear.'

Paddy was remanded to Cork Prison charged with handling stolen goods. Brendan said that the charges would be thrown out when it came to court but that they wanted to put pressure on Paddy by lifting him and remanding him in a prison at a distance from his family and associates.

Hutchie arranged for Lorraine to go to Cork on the weekly prisoner's wives bus from the North, he said it was the only way she would be allowed in. It was a humiliation to sit with these women, these big city prisoners' wives, they were that coarse. When she got there she saw Paddy's wife pulling up in a Lexus and Lorraine knew then that Hutchie was mocking her by making her go on the bus. The wife walked past the prisoners' wives bus looking in the other direction and holding the key fob in her hand with an air which said she was the wife and all others were pretenders, and then when Lorraine tried to get in to see him the prison officers told her that only one person was allowed in to see him and that was usually just the wife and not his tart. Lorraine wept bitter tears on the way back in the bus and would not be consoled. As she got off the driver told her not to take the bus again, didn't she know that some of the women's husbands were in for twenty years and he couldn't have a remand prisoner's girlfriend screeching in the bus for a married man? The driver only had one leg and was friends with Hutchie, and Jean said was there some kind of cripples club where the one-eyed and one-legged met and talked cripple stuff which made Lorraine laugh but for a few weeks she would wake up thinking that there were dragging footsteps on the street behind her.

Seventeen

Brendan showed her a letter Paddy had sent to him from prison. There was an inky stamp at the top of the page, Cork Prison Censored, she wondered what that job was like reading all those lonely words of men imprisoned. There would be sex words, little coded phrases. Jean told her that wives and girlfriends pressed the paper to their secret places before they put it in the envelope. *Can you smell me?* Lorraine said don't be disgusting but she wondered if she could be a censor sat in a bare office late at night, a single bulb burning, the night scented with women.

'Are you still with him?' Brendan said. 'A married man's a bad habit. I'll give you forty pounds for every day you stay away from him. It'll be easier than you think. Stay away from him and find yourself a pleasant young man. Think about it and come back to me.'

She was offended that Brendan would think her capable of abandoning Paddy for forty pounds a day or any amount. Brendan left the room and she took the letter from the desk and put it in her handbag and thought of it all day, the paper that Paddy had touched in his lonely cell.

Dear Brendan how are things out there. I just thought Id drop you a few lines as its sunday here and we have plenty of time on our hands. Well first of all i want to thank sweeney for coming up

tell larry also. he can drop me a line if there's any queries regarding anything. you need not show him this letter. I wonder how they got on with that business that I had arranged with your wee man. Any word from him? Did he come to see you. What do you think of this business Brendan that i'm supposed to be involved in. i think it might be a good idea to try and get proof of where i was between those dates that were mentioned. what did you think of that barrister. I suppose he'd be good enough for the trial

I meant too have a chat with you the last

Cork Prison was a closed medium security prison, formerly a military barracks. Paddy's letter is written in blue biro on yellow, lined jotter paper. Punctuation and grammar are erratic but this

143

has no effect on the tone and authority of the letter. The shift of focus is often abrupt and breathless as if spoken or written by a child. But the letter is not written by a child.

The first lines of greeting are casual. *how are things out there.* The prison joke *plenty of time on our hands*, one old friend writing to another, a little wry, a little wistful, how did we get here? It appears that way at first glance but the rest of the letter is to the point. The greeting has no real meaning except to soften the tone so that the censor will be slower to pick up the real intent.

The tone changes abruptly. *Well first of all.* There is an agenda to be completed. He thanks Sweeney for coming up. Sweeney is referred to by his second name but Larry's first name is used. *tell larry also.* Tell him what? It might mean that Brendan was to thank Larry as well as thanking Sweeney for coming up. But it doesn't seem likely. Paddy's grammar and punctuation seem weak but he articulates his meaning clearly. And then *you need not show him this letter.* The word *letter* underlined for emphasis you would think, but then why not underline *need not*? Why would Brendan show Larry the letter and why is he forbidden to do so? The phrasing is formal. *need not.* The peremptory tone. Then the *wee man.* What was to be done between the wee man, Sweeney, Larry and Brendan?

i think it might be a good idea to try and get proof of where I was. In tone it is close to a direction and this characterizes the letter.

Lorraine had thought that Brendan possessed the authority in the relationship between the two men but this letter doesn't read like that. It is a series of instructions to Brendan. *tell larry . . . you need not . . . i meant too have a chat with you. any word* from *the wee man? did he come to see you.* Paddy's in charge. Brendan's not a man to be told what to do. It's one of the reasons Brendan finds himself cast adrift, bankrupt and in the margins of his own and others' lives. So there has to be another reason and the only reason there could be is that Brendan owes Paddy money.

this business . . . that i'm supposed to be involved in. This sentence is not straightforward. It suggests that Paddy is on remand due a series of events or happenings, not some single event such as an assault or a robbery. You know that the *proof* that Paddy is seeking does not in fact exist. The sentence is an invitation to Brendan to start manufacturing the proof, creating alibi witnesses, a trail of false sightings and testimonies.

The letter ends with an offhand and disinterested reference to his barrister. The inference is that one barrister is much the same as another and his job was to play the cards that Paddy and Brendan deal him. It isn't the first defence barrister Paddy has dealt with. He's an old hand with courtroom lawyers and he doesn't really give a fuck about any of them. This is not a document to be read as much as one to be fallen through, a crafted, allusive piece of writing, some lyric fragment from a book of lies.

*

Lorraine pined for Paddy when he was in prison. When there was talk of him getting bail she wanted to drive down in the Peugeot 307 and pick him up but no, it had to be the wife in a BMW. She was as open-minded as the next girl but it tormented her to think of him returned to another, even if she was his wife. She read articles in *Cosmopolitan* about how to spice up your sex life but it seemed beyond her in some deep imagined and unwholesome place. She had seen the girls on the canal bank and the lorry parks in Manchester wearing fake fur coats and short skirts and Paddy said how cold they looked shivering in the winter night and she laughed and he said he felt sorry for them, there were dangerous men out there, perverts and worse. She thought of herself in a stranger's car, pressed against vinyl seats looking up into the face of a man with hurting eyes. She thought of herself for sale in the lorry parks and back alleys of England. Paddy said it was just business but Lorraine wondered how it could be business when the flesh was involved if not the heart, but still she knew they would fuck like thieves when he got out, God forgive her, she would fuck him bendy when she got him to herself.

Eighteen

You didn't often see Nora outside the Bureau, never mind stood at Lorraine's flat door with her finger on the bell. She looked smaller, there were pulled threads on her tweed suit, some small harried figure you'd see in Newry market.

'It's all gone,' Nora said when Lorraine opened the door.

'What do you mean?'

'All the American Express money is gone.'

'How can it be gone?'

'Mr Carney.'

'What has Carney got to do with it?'

For several months the building contractor Carney had changed a cheque for in the tens of thousands every Monday. It was a classic mark. The cheque was honoured every time, softening up the victim. When Carney wanted to change more,

Brendan did not see anything wrong although he should have. When Carney cashed a second cheque for the same amount on Tuesday Brendan should have delayed the payout at least until the first cheque had cleared but he did not. And when a third cheque was presented on Wednesday he should have known that cheques had a three-day cycle and that Carney was about to take everything that he had.

Carney had worked on large construction sites and he had shown Brendan logbooks for plant and machinery that he owned. Road graders, twenty-ton tracked machines which were kept in a border compound in Killeavy. When Carney's cheques bounced Brendan sent Hutchie and Owen out to inspect the machinery Carney had used as collateral. The machines were lined up in a defile. They had been there for years, the scarred machines sunk in the mud with cracked hydraulic lines and fractured tracks, windows broken, briars growing through the chassis, tyres flat.

'Scrap. Your da isn't going to like this,' Hutchie said. 'He isn't going to like this one fucking bit.'

Nora said that Brendan started to decline after the Carney fraud. He had always been a gambler but now the bets were high and reckless. She saw cloth bags of cash being carried into Hughes Bookmakers, and she saw little of it being carried out again. The mosaic horses and their little jockeys were covered in road dirt and no one bothered cleaning them. There were rumours of bets in the tens of thousands. Brendan was spending more time in McCrink's. People still came to him there with their legal problems but when they had spoken to him they left him alone at a table in the corner where he drank and smoked Silk Cut reds as though he had been given a task to complete, some ashen command that must be fulfilled. Nora sent in sandwiches and arranged for a taxi to bring him home across the border at night but that was all that could be done. And when he had bet on a race and the race was showing on the television above the bar, the horses plunging towards the line in midwinter mud and rain, Brendan did not watch. You knew the outcome of the race to be preordained and your bet either lost or won before he had put your money down.

Lorraine could now clearly see the difference between Brendan and the others. Dominic and Mary belonged in the present and the future. There was no past. There could not be because it would be acrid with the sound of gunshots and women crying for their men. Brendan was different, left shifty by memory. Jean would go off and leave Brendan at the bar where he would drink quietly on his own. Lorraine knew Brendan didn't love Jean and that it didn't matter. Jean had told her that Brendan had always wanted a daughter. He didn't have to say it, Jean said, all men want a daughter, someone to love them beyond reason, and girls craved the love of a father like a wound. She wondered if Brendan had offered to bribe his wife for a girl, *If we have a girl I'll pay you*, and how much that payment might be in the currency of husbands and wives. Brendan told Jean that if he had a girl she would be called Jacqueline after Jackie Kennedy. There were books in Brendan's office on the Kennedys and on the assassination of John Kennedy in Dallas. Was that what Brendan wanted for her, Black Jack's daughter, a bayou girl sent to Vassar, all of her grace bent to a man's will? Did he wish for his daughter sunglasses and a Dior suit, just for a moment to carry that beauty and terror and longing in a dusty sunstruck plaza?

Bann said he wondered about Brendan. That the mind was not what it had been, that the clutch was slipping but in fact it was Bann's clutch that was slipping, he had been admitted to hospital twice with pneumonia but he made light of it and said that it was best treated with tincture of rum.

Nineteen

Muirhevnamor is a large local authority estate on the flatlands to the south of Dundalk, seven miles from the border. It was built in the early 1970s, and housing there was allocated to local families and to refugees from the North who had crossed the border in the early seventies. The native deprived and those dispossessed in other places for other reasons were put side by side, and how do you see into the heart of such places, subject to sea breezes and estuary mist from the coastal mudflats to the east?

When Dominic was imprisoned following the shoot-out at Foynes, Mary took the boys to live in Slieve Foy Park in Muirhevnamor. The daughter she had been seen with at the border as she waited for Dominic's extradition had died of meningitis at eighteen months. Police said that Mary lived a quiet life when Dominic was in prison but quiet was alien to Mary and her like.

On Saturday, 2nd February, Mary was running a bath for the boys in the upstairs bathroom. A cold evening, early dark, coal smoke hanging in the lit entries and avenues of the estate. There was condensation on the bathroom windows, the television on in the living room. The back door opened onto a yard and then an alley. Two men wearing hoods and carrying firearms entered from the alley, walked through the yard and opened the unlocked back door. They are calm. They have done this kind of thing before, they are children of the border heir to carnage. They walk past the first boy and then the second and they cross the hallway and they climb the stairs. Mary hears her boys call and she knows what is coming. A child's voice at such a time. What is to be written of this moment for she is herself known to death and recognizes that the bargains to be completed in these moments are bargains for eternity. She cries out to them not to kill her, for who would not ask? But they will not leave without the blood they came for. Mary backs into the bathroom and the men pass through and stand side by side and raise their weapons and fire into her. Then they stoop and pick up the brass shell casings, ensuring the number of fired rounds is counted. Then they leave the house. One of the boys ran to a neighbour's house to fetch help. The neighbour found Mary dead in the bathroom, her head in the bath. She had been shot nine times in the face. It was said that the bullet holes were in the shape of a cross.

Everything points to the shooting as revenge for the deaths of Eric Dale, Eamon McMahon and Mackin. Police sources say that the file on Mary McGlinchey's murder remains open but admit that it is unlikely that charges will ever be brought.

At the time of her death police in the North had been seeking to interview Mary in relation to twenty killings. Of Dominic's reaction in prison to Mary's death nothing is written. What did he say or do when they came to him to say that Mary is dead in her motherhood, in her connivance, in her mannish beauty, in her love and cruelty? When news of her death was relayed to Portlaoise Prison it was decided to let him sleep for the night before he was woken and moved from the wing he occupied to a solitary cell. The prison authorities said Dominic requested leave to attend her funeral but they would not release him from prison. Authorities offered him a private service within the precincts of the gaol but he turned it down. Mary McGlinchey. We do not know who we are when we are living and we remain undiscovered when we are dead.

Nora told Jean that there was money coming through the Bureau that she had never seen before. Big money in cash and cheques, one hundred thousand a day and more. And Nora said that the only people who had that kind of money in cash were three or four cross-border smugglers and drug dealers. The money was turned over fast, Brendan converting the cash and writing a cheque. He had found another form of gambling, a purity to it. But he was losing money on every transaction. It was a pyramid scheme, Nora said, and it could not go on for ever. Jean told Lorraine and asked her to talk to Paddy.

'This isn't the fucking Salvation Army he's dealing with here,' Jean said. 'I'm scared.'

Lorraine had never heard of a pyramid scheme before, but it felt like something to do with the boy princes in their silent tombs and therefore with death and an ornamented passage into it.

Lorraine didn't want to talk to Paddy but Jean kept on at her until she asked him. Paddy shook his head.

'The only thing I can think of is that he's done some kind of a deal with the oil boys,' he said, 'but I can't see what it is. You'd want to be staying clear of Brendan for a while. And Jean too.'

Hutchie said that Brendan was only trying to make back the money he had lost to Carney and not to mind him but Hutchie was already making plans to bail out and it would suit him to see Brendan go down.

Jean said that Brendan had done a lot for her and she would not desert him in his hour of need, but Hutchie said that Jean just wanted to wring every last red cent she could out of him while he still had it.

'You'll see,' he said. 'The day and hour the bubble bursts you won't see our Miss Jean for dust.'

No one doubted that things would go wrong soon. Paddy wouldn't let Lorraine go into the Bureau any more, but sometimes when she was driving down Water Street the door of McCrink's bar would open and she would see Brendan sitting on his own at the table in the corner, his cigarettes and drink in front of him. Sometimes in these years it was hard to tell one foreboding from another but this time it was clear. Brendan was cheating dangerous men out of their money and there would be consequences. No one mentioned it but the day that the cheques written to the smugglers were returned unpaid from the bank in Trevor Hill they remembered Eamon dead and locked in the boot of his own car and left on the border.

Twenty

Paddy was held for four months until the High Court granted him bail. Paddy said that the charges were spurious and that he was an innocent man. Paddy was careful to remain within the law in small matters. His cars were always taxed and insured and in good mechanical condition, including the old ones he used when he didn't want to draw attention to himself. Don't give them a reason to look closer, he said. That's all they need. He had some cover in that regard but it was different for the others, Dominic could not hide who he was. He was an outlaw and did outlaw things. Brendan had been a lawyer and regarded lawkeepers in this time of war as mediocre and compromised, there to be played, there to be outfoxed.

The first night Lorraine met Paddy after prison she felt like she hardly knew herself. The lace-marked skin was not hers, the heels chafed in black patent stilettos, the narrow bra straps that cut into your shoulders. Who was this girl, lip-glossed and wearing lace gloves that reached to her elbows, the girl she held in her head and not the one she saw in the mirror who had a shopworn mystique at best?

'Brendan's the smartest man I ever met,' Paddy said, 'but sly is a different thing, and there's many a man is slyer than him and he pays no heed to them and that's his downfall. That and the drink.'

Paddy and Lorraine did not drink much, nor did Dominic and Mary. Brendan and Hutchie did enough drinking for all of them, Brendan in particular.

This border life could not be sustained. Paddy and Brendan knew it, Paddy better than Brendan, and he started to buy property to legitimize his business. But your deeds track you down and they had all made themselves in blood and consequence there was no recusing from it.

Paddy had bought a good house in Newry. It felt like old money. The houses were Victorian villas, set back from the road on a height looking over Newry docks to Carlingford Lough and the mountains beyond.

The neighbours were doctors, pharmacists. Lorraine saw what he was trying to build for himself and knew it was a lie.

She knew it was always Paddy and her crossing the border, the desperado and his girl. You went hard down these roads, rushing to meet whatever the night might throw up to you. The sooner you met trouble the sooner you were out the other side of it but when Paddy bought the house Lorraine would drive up to and sit outside in her car on the road looking up at it with the suburban light in the big bay windows, dusk the sweetest hour.

Lorraine was always on at Paddy to go on holidays with her. She asked Paddy if he would take her to Graceland. She thought Paddy would like it the way he liked big new pubs in the suburbs and people flush with cash but Paddy said he was ill-fitted for a visit to a mausoleum and Lorraine said well you've no problem with Florida when half of them's at death's door. Lorraine did not see as Paddy did that death could come at you in stealthful and tawdry ways and he knew it would be present in the mould-ering passageways and southern glooms of Graceland. Paddy could see real estate opportunities in Florida, long unshadowed vistas, sea lit condos, the light flooded dreaming of a man who thinks he sees a way out.

They drove to England for the next trip. They missed the last ferry and Paddy took her to a hotel in Larne close to the ferryport. There were long empty corridors, bedrooms with flock wallpaper. You could hear the big freighters in the North Channel, the foghorns and the East Maiden light when the

channel was fogbound and the mile-long light showed you on
the bed, the shadow of a man above you, looking down on your
ghastly pale and cheapened self. When they had finished she
went out onto the balcony. She stood against the balcony rail
and looked out at the freight yards below and the sea beyond it.
How you worked for a man, the task of yourself, undressed on
a bedspread. She wanted to ask him is this how you want me,
in a rundown hotel room sprawled on a bed, the sheets stained?

They stopped at services in Warrington, and Paddy went inside
to pay for petrol. Paddy often left Lorraine out of the light,
always finding the boundaries in places, always taking her into
the cold where the shadows lay, keeping her away from the
belonging places, the house, the well-lit rooms.

She put her hand in the glove compartment. You did things
like that with Paddy. This life made you a sneak. You looked
in coat pockets, desk drawers, all the places where the world
kept itself hidden. Things he touched took on the patina of
evidence. You thought of them as bagged and labelled, pored
over. She found matchbook covers from bars she had never
been to, Florida hotel receipts, you never knew where he had
been, you never knew who had been with him. The forensics
of himself. He could make you believe that it was something
he did for you, revealing what was untrustworthy in you, the
knowledge that you were broken. You were a skulker in pockets,

made a spy in your own house. There was a matchbook from the Black Cat Club. She thought of women in hostess uniforms, vixens in short dresses.

A thin girl left the place she had been standing close to the petrol pumps. She was wearing a white imitation leather miniskirt and white knee boots and a short black bolero jacket. The light caught her face and high cheekbones and the acne scars in her cheeks which seemed hollowed out, graven with loss.

There had been a look or a remark between the thin girl and Paddy. Lorraine saw it as Paddy came back to the car, he lifted his head and the girl seemed to turn her head to the side, it was hard to tell but sometimes these were all the things you had to go on, what was half glimpsed in passing car headlights and bar-room mirrors and other night ephemera. Lorraine got out of the car.

'If you look at my man like that again I'll scrab them baby blues out of your head.'

'You and whose army, darlin'?' the girl said. She was smiling.

'Don't you smile like that at me, miss.'

The girl's teeth were crooked, her face and mouth shadowed into a grimace. Paddy came over. 'Get back in the car, Lorraine.'

'Think tha's less common than me,' the girl said, her eyes moving between Paddy and Lorraine. 'Looks to me tha's doing the same job as us.'

'You shut your dirty mouth,' Lorraine said.

'I'd take spitfire home, mister, and get her fixed. She's not right.'

'Get in the car, Lorraine.'

'Is that what I am to you? Just business. Like her?' She felt tense, pinched and mean. 'You think I'm like them, don't you?'

'I don't know what you're talking about.'

'Used goods. You think you can buy me. A frock and a fancy hotel.'

She didn't speak on the way to the ferry. Paddy put a Slim Whitman cassette in the deck. There were lost places in the world. Trailing him through the margins of the known world. Men and women in the pre-dawn, the fen mist drifting through the petrol station lights, young women drift like ghosts of the twenty-first century, as if it had already happened and left these afterimages, the grey-blue negative of themselves trailing Lorraine through the margins of the known world. They take their place in the queue for the ferry, they're the newest car there, all else are rusted worn-out vehicles, cracked windscreens, the seats worn to the nap. Everyone's pale and tired.

Lorraine goes to the bathroom on the ferry. She sees the blonde girl as a visitant from the city girls of long ago at Giles Quay with their king size cigarettes and paper bags smeared with Evo-Stik, giving themselves up to be handled and groped at the back of the caravan site toilet block, there was always a smell of the sea, rank mud and weed from the dredged up spoil of the lough. She looks in the mirror and she knows what she is now. She is a minx, a moll, a sloven, a siren. What else could she be? Now naked save for a black bra, her pale flesh moving in the darkened bedroom? She is giving herself up to be devoured, padding towards the tied man in the bedroom, the air rank with sex and the death to come.

Twenty-One

Jean said that Brendan's wife was a lady like Nora. She played bridge and gave coffee mornings for other wives. Jean wouldn't hear a word against her even though as Lorraine told Paddy Jean was having 'a physical relationship' with Elizabeth's husband. Jean seemed to think that she shared something with Elizabeth but Lorraine knew Elizabeth would not have given Jean the time of day. Lorraine didn't say anything to Jean but she allowed herself a small smile any time that Jean mentioned it, and when Jean saw the smile she knew the meaning and she didn't speak to Lorraine for weeks on end. Lady Muck, she told Hutchie, that's who she thinks she is. If that's the case, Hutchie said, there's two of you in it and neither of you much of a lady, to be fair.

When Jean told Brendan about what Lorraine had said he put cash behind the counter for her in Snaubs boutique in Newry.

'That's Brendan's answer to everything,' Jean said. 'He'd buy you or bribe you or bet you out from under yourself.'

Brendan told her that she was as much a lady as anyone.

'Don't lie to me,' Jean said. 'I know what I am.'

Lorraine had become a daily mass-goer in these years. They all knew it but no one said anything. She kept a missal on the hall table in the flat with white gloves folded on top. She had been brought up in the Church, had received the sacraments of baptism and had made her first communion with the other children of her class wearing a white dress and veil. There was something sexual in the figure of Christ but you couldn't say it aloud or even think it. The loincloth draped on the angled hips, the piercing in his left side, the lipped wound.

Monks of the Redemptorist order brought a mission to her secondary school. Gaunt men dressed in brown robes, roped at the waist with a large wooden crucifix thrust into the rope. A metal figure of Christ was affixed to the crucifix, the Christ figure gaunt and tormented. You wanted to reach out and touch the rib slats, the swart jawed face drawn with pain.

They spoke of the agonies in Christ's face, agonies of thirst, of spear thrust and the driven nail. Agonies of betrayal. Imagine the grains of sand on the beach, they said, and multiply them, and that is only the start of eternity. Be it known to you children that the walls of hell are seven thousand miles thick. Be you aware of the worm that shall not die, the fire that shall not be quenched, the agony that will not end. Be not deceived. The devil has his lures and entrapments and these are the very pleasures you are drawn to, the signposts to an eternity of torment.

She would have known the Church's law against suicide, austere and catechistic. *We are stewards, not owners, of the life that God has given us.* She would have known that suicides were forbidden funeral mass and burial on consecrated ground. She would know that those who took their own lives placed themselves beyond forgiveness, in mortal sin, the separation of the self from God for eternity. There would be a solitary windswept grave outside the cemetery wall. She would have known that if she took her own life, then all of her would be of no avail. That even the piteous starveling Christ wouldn't be for her but still she took a man's life and then took her own.

She knew she was guilty of breaking the Sixth Commandment. Turning the word *adulterer* over in her mind, seeing herself as haggard and sinful. Lorraine making peace in those early morning masses in unheated and almost empty chapels, the mumbled rituals. If the other mass-goers, the scarfed women and old men, noticed her in her blonde highlights and nails they said nothing.

You return to her actions that week. The letters left behind. The buying of the shotgun and her purchase of a double grave. The theatre of her own death. It feels over plotted. An evidential trail is laid. Murder suicides do not often exhibit this degree of certainty. Suicide notes are not uncommon but they do not take you into the last unwitnessed moments. Lorraine was said to be *in good form* in the week leading up to her death. The suicidal state of mind is said to present this way in the last weeks, the last days or hours. The decision has been made. The weight has been lifted. Towards Jesus and his dark sinewed body you raise your yearning heart.

Twenty-Two

On his release from prison Dominic appeared diminished. He took a part-time job in a supermarket in Drogheda. He was described as a broken man following the killing of his wife, although police said that during this period he had been involved in armed robberies in and around Drogheda. One assassination attempt had been made. A car had pulled up alongside his car and a man had got out and approached Dominic. At first Dominic assumed it was a plainclothes policeman but the gun the man carried was an old-model Sten sub-machine gun and Dominic knew that the Special Branch carried Israeli Uzis. Dominic grappled with the man and the gun went off leaving a bullet lodged in Dominic's skull. The men escaped. Dominic said afterwards that the gunman and the driver had English accents. They were never found, nor were the men who were to kill Dominic.

Dominic had told Vincent Browne that he did not expect to die in bed, but there is a world between such statements and being sprawled in a purge of blood on a February street beaten and shot fourteen times. Dominic and his son had driven from Brookville Estate on the Drogheda North Quay to Hardman's Gardens where Dominic stopped to make a call from a phone box.

Children in parkas walked the streets in the cold, hunched into their hoods, monkish in the pale streetlight they seemed in procession to chant tenebrae.

The North Quay roads pitted, torn up. There was a sense of aftermath. Solitary men on the quay looking like lone survivors, empty-eyed and trudging.

There were rust stains in the cobbles where the train lines had run to the dockside. Driving past the cast-iron crane mountings intact on the dockside. The cogged and seized wheel of a rail turntable.

The person he was to call was not traced, one more ghost voice. A red Mazda pulled up on the other side of the street and three men got out. The men were unmasked and indifferent to the presence of multiple witnesses on the street.

Hardman's Gardens was on the opposite side of the hospital to Boyle O'Reilly Terrace a few minutes' walk away and contiguous to St Peter's with its cadaver tombs and ghastly beheaded priest in his catafalque and the house where Lorraine and Paddy died. You look for the summons that brought both Paddy and Dominic to these empty streets, but sometimes you look for order where there is none. The priest's tongueless mouth has been silent for centuries.

Witnesses said that the men beat Dominic to the ground, then opened fire with pump-action shotguns. One of them then shot him in the head. Before he died Dominic said, *Jesus, Mary help me.*

Before the police arrived Dominic's sixteen-year-old son knelt beside his father's body and emptied his pockets, taking scraps of paper, receipts, anything that might be useful to investigators. Don't leave them anything, Dominic had said. Even a petrol receipt can tell them a hundred things, where you were, what time you were there. They talk to garage people and shop people and find out who you were with. The boy had never thought about this before, the trails we leave in the world, it felt like something bright to him, arcing off into the hours and days of your being, people might try to follow you into yourself, to insert themselves in your present.

The state pathologist, Professor John Harbison, told the inquest into the death of Dominic McGlinchey that he had carried out a post-mortem examination on the body of McGlinchey (42). As Dr Harbison removed the dead man's clothing, three bullets and one bullet case were recovered. X-rays showed Dominic had a bullet in his neck, skull, seven to the left upper-chest area, one in his left arm, one in his left leg and two in his right leg. Fourteen bullets were found and he believed the last bullet to the head was a coup de grâce – 'a final shot to make sure he was dead', the pathologist said.

Hardman's Gardens. Hardman. Now there's a laugh Hutchie said. He wasn't that hard of a man in the heel of the hunt, he had his prayers said before they put a bullet in his head.

Twenty-Three

Brendan told Nora what she already knew. That all his money was gone and so was the money belonging to those who had been profiting from the excessive exchange rates he had offered. All the cheques he had written had been returned unpaid. Nora said nothing of what took place between them on that morning, for who was she to repeat the words of a fallen man? She had brought a display of roses from her garden when she came to work and she put them on the counter in a chipped vase given to her by one of the market traders, knowing they would wither and die in a day or two for no one bar herself would think to water them.

The consequences were felt by the diesel launderers in their underground bunkers ankle deep in sludge and toxic by-product.

It was felt in Jonesborough market by the sellers of bootleg vodka and smuggled cigarettes. Those who trafficked in livestock bringing unmarked lorries across the border at night. Importers of illegal fireworks, black marketeers and dealers in false dockets and unearned subsidies and cash instruments meant to evade Excise and Revenue.

Close to £700,000 was missing in the final tally. It was thought unlikely that Brendan could have lost so much money on horses. It was known that Brendan had worked as a temporary clerk in a bank before he became a solicitor. There was talk of shadow banking, accounts in Monaco, in Spain and the Caymans.

'He wasn't fucking gambling with money,' Speedy said, 'he was gambling with his life.'

Speedy was all amphetamine rush and hash comedowns most of the time but he could be clear-headed.

'He can gamble away with his own life,' Hutchie said. 'It's when he starts gambling with mine that I get worried.'

'He's gone deep. He's gone fucking deep this time,' Corrigan said.

'Can you not help him?' Lorraine said.

'He's gone beyond my helping,' Corrigan said. 'Things won't settle down until the money is found and the money won't be found. What can I get you ladies to drink, something strong and sweet?'

'Two Bacardis, one Diet Coke,' Lorraine said.

'Sharing a Diet Coke's not going to help,' Jean said, then was sorry she said it. Lorraine had strange ideas sometimes and was churchy, but there was no real bad in her. She would deny herself, do penance in small things to show she wished good on others.

'As far as I know Brendan hasn't been abroad this past few years, but the son has. Any idea where he might have went?' Corrigan said.

'If I knew I wouldn't fucking tell you, ye slippery bastard,' Jean said.

'That's enough now,' Corrigan said, 'that's enough. I'm doing my best to help here. I couldn't clean up after him this time. He's gone too far.'

'Then what the fuck are you for?' Paddy said.

'If you want to help go into that bookies next door,' Jean said, 'and ask him what he done with the money that Brendan lost on the horses.'

'Hard to believe that that amount of money could be lost gambling and no one knowing about it.'

'It is my belief that is what happened,' Nora said. 'He was deeply upset by the business with the builder.' Nora was loyal to Brendan and would not speak Carney's name. 'It affected him badly. He thought he could recover what he had lost.'

'He was no better judge of a man than he was of a horse if you take a look at the ragtag around him, saving your presence, ma'am.'

'You've no need to save my presence, Mr Corrigan.'

'Then I won't. You were sat here watching him so what did he do with the fucking money?' Nora stood up. Her flower-patterned dress was faded, gone soft with washing. She had a silk scarf around her neck. Her wool cardigan was frayed at the sleeves and elbows. She had a brooch at her throat and Lorraine wondered if she had always worn it and if so why had she not noticed it before. Nora looked as if she had newly come from a decayed country house, a place of the dead, its rooms long silent, and was now called back to it, not to return.

'You are a dishonest and ignorant man, Mr Corrigan. Good afternoon.' They watched her leave.

'She's some woman to be talking about honesty in this place,' Corrigan said, 'and working for that bent fucker Brendan.'

'Nora is a lady,' Bann said.

'And you're a rum-soaked old cunt,' Corrigan said.

This was a border debt owed in blood, and everyone associated with Brendan lay low. Hutchie's phone rang out. Lena wasn't to be seen in Snaubs. There were no Saturday nights in the Imperial and the Lorne was being watched. An unknown man sat at the bar in McCrink's all night, a single drink in front of him. Paddy's house did not change but it took on a shuttered look and no lights were seen on at night. When he was there the Mercedes was parked out the back. There was talk about late night visits to Brendan's house in Ravensdale by men who were owed money. Cars that drove up and stopped outside with headlights on and engines running before driving away. Brendan's wife went to stay with family in England.

Nora had tried to warn the family what was happening. She had done all she could.

Brendan kept the Bureau open in the days following the fraud although no one walked through the door. It would not have been wise for him to be seen on the streets and Jean thought that he was sleeping on the premises. Many customers had lost money and others were too afraid to enter the building, but Owen stayed with him. Brendan spent the day in the back office on the phone. Sometimes a tourist came in to change a traveller's cheque. As the afternoons wore on McCrink's would send in a tray with brandy and ginger and take the empties. Owen and Brendan smoked and did not speak. The silence was not companionable. There was nothing to be said. There had to be a next move but it was not theirs to make and all they could do was wait.

A week after the bank froze the Bureau accounts a man walked in to say that he had accidentally driven into the rear wing of Brendan's car and would Owen inspect the damage? When Brendan came out of the back room Owen had gone outside. He went after him but it was too late. As Owen bent to inspect his father's car the man who had called him out and another man forced him into the back seat of a Granada and a third man drove them in the direction of the border. A mute from High Street known as the Dummy, who collected glasses in McCrink's, had witnessed the struggle. Owen had kicked out and broken off the wing mirror of the car before he was overcome. When Brendan asked the Dummy what he had done, the man mimed picking up the wing mirror from the ground and handing it over to one of the men.

It is not known where Brendan went or who he spoke to in those hours following his son's abduction. He would have had no illusions about the men who had taken him and their belief that the son could stand for the sin of the father, one as good as the other.

'They don't like to be taken for fools,' Hutchie said. But he was wrong. They didn't care whether they were taken for fools or not. They were portrayed in media along the border and further afield as dealers in death and worse. They didn't care about being seen as fools. They only cared about their money.

It was an episode that could only be pieced together in hallucinatory fragments. The boy forced onto the floor of the car. He did not lack courage, otherwise he would never have stood behind the desk of the Bureau knowing that the building was being watched. What he did lack, the Bureau people said, was the wit to run when he could, to see what was in his father's eyes and in the intentions of others. That death did not come for the jaded and the broken. There was nothing to be had there.

He was taken to a location on the border, he did not know if it was north or south and in this deep border country it didn't matter. Jean rang Nora. What will happen to him? Nora was silent but she knew Owen had gone to be held to account in the court of fathers. And her opinion was that he would never come back from it, for there was no verdict of innocence in that assize.

You want to think that Brendan used everything up in the next forty-eight hours. That he went to see the bent cops and the corrupt judges. He did not know many of the politicians but he knew the people who knew the politicians, the handlers and tallymen and perhaps he talked to them. He went to see the journalists. The ones he knew were degraded and often broken and had no influence but you went to see them anyway, then to see the fathers of paramilitaries, men he had represented when they were young and before courts, having been taken from their beds during the night and beaten by soldiers. That he said to them speak to your sons of my son.

He drove into country yards and corrugated sheds stacked to the roof with illicit goods. He went to the houses of men who had threatened him in the past. He had many contacts, and these contacts were interlocking and fragile things. You had to play one off against the other and make them believe that your influence appeared greater than it actually was. To go to them at the same time was to expose yourself and lose all and he lost all.

Brendan could not throw himself upon their decency and likewise mercy for they had none. What plea could be entered in this court? Others had gone to the border to plead for the lives of their loved ones. Wives had asked for the return of husbands, mothers for their sons, and all to no avail. The only possible conclusion is that in his dealings with these men and women over the years he had held something back. That he held some knowledge that might have brought them down. He had rigged the jury for Devine. In the end Devine was a blowhard but his wife was not. You like to think that he went to see Faye Devine in her big house and went on his knees to her.

Twenty-Four

Paddy told Lorraine not to come near the Bureau, that Owen had been abducted and that the police were lifting everybody who might know what had happened to him. Lorraine went to the chancel shop in St Peter's and bought a lace mantilla. She took a candle and lit it in front of the altar and said prayers for Brendan's abducted son.

When she came out of the chapel Paddy was waiting for her. He took her to Brendan's house in Ravensdale to find the rest of the passports. She said what about Elizabeth, Brendan's wife, but Paddy said there had been threats and Brendan's wife had left the house. It was a new house with a large garden now overgrown and French doors on the road side of the house. Paddy parked to the side of the garage and turned off the engine. Lorraine was not afraid of the dark but she was afraid of the empty house and unlit windows and prowled quiet with ivy and uncut shrubberies encroaching on walls and paths.

'What's so important about passports anyhow?'

'They're worth money to the right people.'

'And who are these right people anyway? Can they not get their own passports?'

'Not blank ones. They used to apply for them under dead children's names, just pick the name out of the paper and bring the forms in the child's name to Corrigan and he would sign for them.'

'What's Corrigan got to do with it?'

'You have to get a policeman to sign a passport form.'

'That's terrible, Paddy. That's a terrible thing to do. Why would Corrigan do that?'

'For money. What else would he do it for? So better if I find these ones.'

'Don't leave me out here on my own,' she said.

'You can come in with me,' he said.

'That's near worse,' she said, and she was right but she came with him. The electricity in the house had been disconnected. Paddy had a hand torch. The places men brought you, she thought, the deserted houses and empty rooms of themselves.

They went around the back. French doors opened onto a patio. Leaves had gathered in the patio flagstones. The doors were shabby, paintwork peeling, the wood buckled around the lock and it gave when Paddy put his shoulder against it.

'We shouldn't be here doing this, Paddy.'

'Brendan won't mind.'

'It's not that.' It had nothing to do with Brendan. The permissions withheld in the shadows of this house were not his but those of his family.

'Give me the torch.' She moved the beam around the walls, bare with lighter patches where pictures had been removed. Most of the furniture was gone. There were small piles of clothes, books, scattered papers. What leads a man to this, she thought, that you would ransack your own house?

She picked up a photograph, black and white, the edges foxed and damp spotted. It showed a young Brendan with his arm around Owen. The boy was five or six and was wearing shorts and a striped T-shirt. They were in a city, London she thought, Trafalgar Square, and there were pigeons wheeling about them. Paddy took the torch. She followed him, the torch moving on the plunder of lives, what a house looks like when it is abandoned, mildew on the kitchen cupboards, dank odours. Paddy stopped and switched off the torch. She could see a car's headlights through the trees lining the road twenty yards away. It seemed to slow down, then drive off.

In the photograph the boy stands tight to his father and the man has his arm around him. Owen's toes are turned in, he's a little bit knock-kneed and smiles with his eyes almost closed. He looks nervous, afraid of the pigeons, that's why he edges in closer to the father and the man puts his arm around him. There's always something verminous and indifferent about city pigeons. Lorraine sees them as dead, defleshed, wheeling about him in disarticulated flight, some kind of song-clatter of bones stripped bare, the beaks and skull plates, and she knew why the boy was scared, not that they would touch him with their feathers but that they would take him and wheel him away to a place of death.

'I don't like pigeons.'

'What are you talking about pigeons for?'

'Do you think Owen is still alive?'

'There's not many got took the way he got took and came back from it, that's all I can say.'

'Could they come back for somebody else? If they don't get what they're looking for out of him.'

'They might. They're still looking for their money though it's long gone.' Paddy turned the torch on but hooded it with one hand.

'The car's drove off.'

'No it fucking hasn't. Be quiet.'

Lorraine was scared and cold. She didn't know why they were here to steal something from an empty house. She wanted everything to be like the first days with Paddy, feeling steely and determined, outlaw nights with everything at stake, the world against them but emerging from peril, a companionship of movement and risk, arriving home with rich pillage, not this creeping about in forlorn and ill-smelling rooms, burgling the house of a fallen man.

Lorraine opened a drawer. There were two boxes of expensive playing cards in the drawer and a set of bridge pencils with silver tops. She could see herself with other ladies, a silver coffee pot on the sideboard. She took the first box of cards and put it in her pocket.

'Did you find them?'

'No.'

'When I signed the American Express cheques and put the numbers on the back, did the numbers belong to these passports or to the dead children's passports?'

'These passports.'

'Did your wife sign any of the cheques for you and put the numbers of stolen passports on them?'

'No.'

'Did you ever take her into an empty house looking for things that are against the law?'

Lorraine did not know whether she spoke these words or not, nor did it matter. There were headlights on the driveway and what happened next was like a kidnapping and it came back to her afterwards when she thought about Owen. Paddy's sports jacket was over her head and she was being forced across the room. She wanted to scream but she could not. She felt the impact of her body against the kitchen cupboards and the door frame hard enough to leave bruises though it did not hurt at the time. Was this the last thing, the night air on her legs and the cold grass on her feet? She was pushed against the bodywork of the car and cried out.

She could smell Paddy's aftershave in the lining of the jacket and another perfume that she had never noticed on his clothing before, the wife smell, rank, womanish, possessing.

There were men's voices and then the door opened and the jacket was taken from her head. Behind Paddy she could see Corrigan. More than anything in that moment she hated that Corrigan saw her like this with her mascara running down her face and her skirt up around her waist like all the lonely backseat girls.

'Carney's dead,' Corrigan said.

'Shot?' Paddy said.

'He was found in the forest car park with a hose attached to the exhaust pipe. You'd better keep the head down.'

'Why would I keep the head down if he topped himself?' Paddy said.

'Because nobody believes he done it himself,' Corrigan said. Lorraine knew that Carney had robbed Brendan but she felt a tear in her eye at the thought of him alone in the forest and she blessed herself. Corrigan saw the movement.

'I've seen it all now,' he said. 'The Virgin Mary herself praying for the recently deceased. Don't waste your prayers on him. Don't waste your prayers on any of us.'

Ravensdale Forest abutted the border. It was one of several border places where men brought their sins and learned to live with them or not. The forest was old-growth hardwood and thick pine. The military radar and heat detectors on the northern side of the border could not penetrate it. The lower part of it had once been a pleasure park attached to a Palladian house which had burned down a hundred years since. You came across decorative fountains in the undergrowth, the marble chipped and moss-covered. There were bridges of hand-cut limestone. The house and out-offices had been brought down to their foundations and the stone used elsewhere. You looked across the silent, unpeopled imprint of the building to the hilltop military outposts on the other side of the border, These were watchful places. The living and the dead looked on.

Carney had been found in the car park where the main path into the forest began. A hose was connected to the exhaust pipe of the car and fed through the driver's window. It was set up to look as if Carney had taken his own life but Hutchie said that Carney wouldn't have been permitted the luxury of ending himself.

'Believe you me,' he said, 'he was took out. Somebody

brought him there and set it up to look like he done himself with his own hand. Brendan wasn't the only man he cheated. Carney was bogey to the core.'

But when asked how and why and by whom Hutchie turned his glass eye to the questioner, something ruined and obscene in the sightless look which rendered all questions moot.

Twenty-Five

At a point in the road where you could no longer meet police or soldiers the men allowed Owen to sit upright and then they placed a sack over his head. He didn't try to take it off. He had done his fighting. The sack had contained meal and Owen could smell the bone and dried marrow. It was a smell of decay, of falling away from the light, of the grave.

Owen was manhandled across clear ground then a metal door opened, the bottom of it grinding on hardcore. He was put to sit on hay bales. The men did not speak or remove the hood. He knew that he was indoors and in a large open space, one of the border sheds, a loose corrugated sheet somewhere over his head banging in the wind, echoing in the girdered space. He knew he was alone but he did not remove the bag or get up. He could not make his situation better but there were ways he could make it worse. He didn't know what to do with his hands. He let them hang at his sides then he folded them in his lap. They left him alone for several hours, then he heard the door open and he found himself bathed in cold air as though the night itself had come for him.

'Where's the money?'

'The money your da owes us?'

'I don't know anything about it.'

'If you don't tell us we'll bate it out of you.'

'Did he take it abroad? One of them Caymans accounts maybe? The Isle of Man?'

One of the men was angry, one quiet. He knew that one was as dangerous as the other but still you felt the quiet man was looking for something more and that he was the one who would put a gun to your head.

'Did you ever see anything in the house resembling a jury list?'

'Fuck this talk. Let's just send him home and be done.'

Was there a list in the house? Owen said yes there was. There had been a list on the table in the dining room and Brendan had spent long hours over it and then he had gone out and not come home for three days.

What did it say at the top? Did it say Electoral Register? Were there names ticked off on it? Ticked off or struck through. Owen said yes again.

'I'm for sending this sorry bastard home right now.'

'You don't make the call, you could get sent home yourself.'

'That's it. We're fucked. Whatever the fuck he done we can't do nothing now.'

'More fool us that we chanced our money with his da. You fly with the crows you get shot.'

'What'll we do with this one?'

'Get the Hiace.' Owen heard footsteps moving away from him and he thought that the angry one had left. He could hear the other's quiet breathing.

'You know what he meant by sending you home? He didn't mean going back to your ma. He meant your heavenly home, son. He meant a hole blew to fuck in the side of your head and threw by the side of the road for the rats to ate is what he meant.'

The second man left the shed. The wind blew under the door and stirred dust and grains on the floor. Owen sat there for a long time, he had no way of telling how long but it got colder and the starlings that he had heard over his head had ceased to flutter from girder to girder and by that he took it to be night or close to it. He regretted not having tried to lift a corner of the bag earlier to observe the daylight as it might be the last light he got to see.

He sat on in the dark. He had become accustomed to the smells of the bag over his head, the organic reek. There was a smell he feared more. Earth and worm mould.

He did not hear the shed door open but he felt the night cold on his face and then it was gone. There was no footfall but there was a light metallic sound, some jewel or trinketry touched against the corrugated door and he could smell perfume. He knew nothing of perfume but he knew this to be strong because he could smell it despite the bag over his head, a rich fragrance corrupted by the smells in the bag.

There was a chinking as though death came decorated and scented, in bracelets and finery, to take you for its own. Owen thought of asking for mercy but he knew that if there was mercy he would not be here now.

Paddy and Lorraine drove along the edge of the Ravensdale forest to the sea, the winter trees stilled in geometric shapes, the sky graphed in blackness, driven-on and starred road ice catching the headlights, the night in glints and shadows. They didn't speak until they reached the junction for Greenore.

'Take me to the carriage,' Lorraine said.

'It'll be freezing.'

'You won't be cold,' Lorraine said, 'I promise.'

Paddy turned north driving through the cold townlands of Grange and Lordship. He stopped on the beach littoral and turned off the BMW. There was frost to the tideline, crystalline in the sand.

'You had money in the Bureau. Carney took your money as well, didn't he?'

'Brendan had my share of the American Express. I want the passports. It won't pay me back but it'll help.'

'Did youse kill Carney?'

'What do you want to know that for?'

'I want to know what class of man I'm laying with.'

'Nobody killed Carney. He took his own life.'

'Says who?'

'Corrigan.'

'Then there's no reason to doubt him is there?'

'I believe him. Carney robbed the wrong men. He had two choices. He could do it himself or have it done for him.'

'So he done it himself.'

'I don't know what he done except he run out of choices.'

'Is that what happens when you run out of choices?'

Paddy didn't answer. She could see sea mist gathering at the bar and the Blockhouse island. The Haulbowline lighthouse sounded. There were big freighters anchored outside the bar and their lights disappeared one by one.

'Will we go up to the carriage?' she said. Paddy sat with his eyes on the sea and the scant lights of Greencastle on the far shore soon to be lost to the fog and again did not answer. She leaned against his shoulder. She understood that these men required women to fill the house of their silence.

Later when the Haulbowline light passed over their half-undressed bodies she thought is that all we are good for? She knelt up in the bed. He was still awake and he did not move when she bent over him. A fine scar had formed where Paddy's head had been gashed. She bit it, drawing blood. The blood ran down into his eye and pooled in the socket. She bent her mouth to it. There was a law of blood and there was a law of trespass. Nothing could afterwards be the same.

When darkness fell they took Owen from the shed. They kept the bag over his head. He could feel the night fathomless around him. In the distance a bullock roared, the sound carrying over ditches and bents, unechoing so that he knew he was on flat land. There was a tidal odour of decayed wracks and other seaweeds. He thought he might be close to the sloblands of Jenkinstown and Lordship. He could hear men's voices nearby but could not make out what they were saying. He knew that the question of himself would have been dispensed with by now, the matter of his disposal in this world and the next. A diesel engine started. He was pushed towards the sound of the engine and his hands were placed on a jeep tailgate and the vehicle began to move slowly forward. He walked with it, crossing fields of soft marl and river meadow. He felt the jeep lurch down onto a stone stream bed and he forded the water ankle-deep.

They left him in a stubble field with the full moon rising over the transmitter on Ravensdale mountain. He was turned so that he faced away from the direction the jeep would travel and the bag was taken from his head. The jeep drove off into the night and didn't turn on its lights until it had gone through the field gate and onto the road. They'd have as soon left him there dead or alive. It made no difference to them.

He was asked afterwards if anything that had happened in that twenty-four hours had harmed him and he answered truthfully no. He seldom thought about it. He did not wake from sleep with a start. But something was forestalled in him then, another life that he might have had, nothing seemed as much of consequence afterwards. He said that when the bag had been taken from his eyes the cut wheatfield had blazed like fire in the light of the risen moon.

Later that year Joseph Devine was tried for fuel smuggling and tax evasion. Despite overwhelming evidence of guilt the jury found him not guilty. There were rumours of jury tampering and Lorraine wanted to know if it was anything to do with the money she had seen changing hands in the counting room of the Fairways Hotel but they all told her to keep quiet and not to be speaking of such things.

Twenty-Six

Brendan signed himself into St John of God's acute pyschiatric hospital in Dublin. No one knew if something had shifted in his mind or if it was a stratagem to avoid arrest or if it was the only place where he could be safe. Owen and Nora kept the Bureau open. Dried leaves blew in from the street when the door opened, the fluorescent lights flickered and dimmed behind the Money Changed sign. Custom was scant. The market traders came in after nightfall, changed their money and left, and no one entered by the steel door to ask Nora to dance. Bann sat on his bar stool by the wall, although there were few market pick-ups to be made and he was no longer paid, but it was Bann who answered the phone when Brendan rang from the hospital. Bann handed the phone to Owen. Patients in locked wards did not have access to telephones but they knew this would not have deterred Brendan. Some orderly would have been bribed or flattered and in the end persuaded to act against their own interest.

Owen spoke his name and waited. He barely recognized his father's voice. The others sat in silence, the whispery tones of the incarcerated man carrying into the office though his words were not clear. If Bann had been a Catholic he would of blessed himself, Hutchie said afterwards, and done a fucking novena to boot. Owen put the phone down. 'He wants us to go to the hospital.'

'When?'

'Now.'

'Fuck it'll be the middle of the night by the time we get there. Brendan crooks the finger and youse all jump,' Hutchie said but he got into the car with the rest of them. They didn't question Owen. He had gone to what they had assumed was a certain death and had come back and was in their eyes elevated.

They drove down the main road to Dublin through Dundalk and Drogheda. Bann was sitting in the back seat and when Hutchie looked in the mirror all he could see was the whites of Bann's eyes, the alcoholic old fucking ghoul. When they got to the hospital grounds Bann got out with Owen and it was Hutchie who stayed in the car for he'd had enough of looming institutions.

It was a wild night, a named storm on the Irish Sea and the Dublin bar, force ten at the Kish light, the streets and suburbs around John of God's empty and rain-lashed, wisteria and privet tossed and shredded on the walkways and pavements of the hospital. There were small branches and litter caught in the steel mesh fence of the secure unit, rain driven horizontally under the security lights. They would not let Bann enter because he was not a family member and he lit a damp Gold Bond and tried to find shelter in one of the arched gothic window embrasures. There was a new wing to the hospital and behind that the old buildings, the forgotten campuses, bedlamites adrift in the quadrangles.

Brendan was in B Ward, a secure male ward. An orderly buzzed you in and you signed at the desk. There were men in pyjamas, some of them moving about and some of them in bed. A desk with nurses at it. Scuffed charts on the desktop. Liquid medicines in clear plastic cups, the smell of dredged-up toxins. Owen looking up for Brendan every time he heard the padding of slippered feet, men shuffling in hospital gowns, you could see the pale, naked body under the green material, everything here was on the bleak edge of living, far-flung outlands of the mind, shuffling revenants on linoleum corridors.

An orderly pointed him to Brendan's bed. Asked afterwards if his father was lucid, he said you couldn't tell, the place coming back to him in gothic imaginings. Brendan was wearing a dressing gown and slippers and kept his eyes fixed on the bedspread. Once he glanced quickly upwards and Owen caught something glittery in his eyes, deranged, fallen, then it was gone. Brendan took a piece of torn jotter paper from his dressing gown pocket and handed it to Owen. It had been written on in pencil, a rudimentary interior of the hospital building, the handwriting crabbed.

Brendan gestured to the wall behind the metal-framed bed, a movement of his hand that Owen recognized from his upbringing. You were meant to do something but you were not meant to understand it, it was a gesture of petulant command. Owen looked at the door. It did not seem to have been used for years and had been painted over but the old gloss paint which sealed it had been hacked away.

Owen pushed at the door and it swung open onto a service corridor. There were old trolleys, wheelchairs with canvas seats, frayed and stained. Bedside lockers and chairs with their members rotted and broken. The ceiling panels had fallen off exposing wiring ducts and copper piping. Following the map Owen turned left. The corridor was dimly lit, the windows barred and shuttered, although you could hear the storm outside and draughts stirred the cobwebs over his head. A rudimentary staircase had been drawn on the map and he found it at the end of the corridor and climbed it, the wooden steps creaking under his feet and he felt as if he was climbing up and out of the present and into a tale of the past. Far below he heard a man's lunatic howl and another man further away picked it up and howled back, lords of unreason calling him away from his task or urging him onwards he could not tell. The staircase opened onto a landing with metal-framed windows open to the night. The windows flexed in the storm and the metal frames screeched where they touched. Owen saw white shapes floating outside the window and when he went closer he saw that they were seagulls, driven inland by the storm, and despite the force of the tempest they rode the wind and barely moved.

The map directed him to a corridor on the same level. The wooden boards of the corridor had been ripped up to reveal pipes and ducting underneath, worked on then abandoned and left covered in dust. There was a lit room at the end of the corridor. Owen could see a canvas chair in the middle of the room with several brown cardboard files on the seat. He walked down the corridor stepping from joist to joist, testing each one before he put his full weight on it. The door frame of the room was splintered and worm-eaten and again he tested the boards before he put his full weight on them. It might once have been a bedroom, the floral wallpaper was damp and hung away from the wall in strips and there was an iron bedstead in the corner, the frame rust-spotted, broken springs hanging from their fixings, the mattress mildewed and stained. Owen lay down on the mattress. Above him slates rattled and the ceiling plasterwork flexed from the wind blowing through the attics of the building. This would do him as refuge, this room here in the eaves of bedlam, and he stayed there for an hour until the wind died down and then he took up the files and went back along the corridor and down into the ward again. Brendan was sitting in a wing-backed armchair with his eyes closed and he did not open them nor did he appear to be watching for his son. Owen put the files under his arm. The locks were heavy-set, brass-keyed, you could be here for ever. The orderly carried a set of keys at his belt. Owen waited for him to ask about the files under his arm but he did not, for what was there to be smuggled from a mental hospital?

Bann was waiting for him in the rain, coughing and bent double. They put Bann in the front seat of Hutchie's car.

'How was he?' Hutchie said.

'I don't know.'

'How do you not know? How did he look? What did he say?'

'Just told me to get files from the top floor of the building.'

'How the fuck did he get them there? He's supposed to be under lock and key.'

'Leave the boy alone,' Bann said. 'He says he doesn't know.' Bann was shaking and coughing.

'Must have been lucid enough to know the run of the place and to get you into the rest of the building. Those wards are supposed to be secure. Locked down.'

'This is Brendan you're talking about,' Bann said.

'Aye but he's not a ghost can go through walls and locked doors.'

'What's in them anyhow?' Hutchie said.

'I didn't open them.'

'Give us a look.'

'No.'

'The passports. It's the passports isn't it?'

'He never looked, didn't he say that?'

'I think we had better take Mr Bann to a doctor,' Nora said.

'Take me to a bar and set up a rum would suit me better.'

They drove away from the hospital, rain driven across the rear window as Owen looked back through the rain-tossed branches of the boundary trees, the hospital locked down for the night, Brendan not sleeping, the father in him awake and abroad in the corridors and hidden spaces, abroad in the vagrant dark. Picking his way through memory the way you'd pick your way through the streets and avenues of a burned-out city. When they got to the cutstone bridge over the river Fane in Dundalk Owen told Hutchie to stop the car. He got out and walked to the parapet. The river below was in full spate, high tide, the borderland draining into the sea. He threw the file he had taken from the hospital over the parapet and got back into the car. No one said anything. Later when Hutchie told Paddy what had taken place

Paddy didn't say anything, which Hutchie thought was strange until Jean said maybe the fucking passports weren't there in the first place for no one had looked.

Twenty-Seven

A fortnight later Brendan discharged himself from the psychiatric hospital and came back to Newry. He had held on to his old solicitor's office opposite the police barracks in Catherine Street, the building deemed worthless after years of paramilitary attacks on the barracks. The house was damaged outside and derelict inside. The barracks had been mortared several times and the window frames of the office had buckled and there were shrapnel marks on the render. Inside several ceilings had collapsed and the laths were exposed. There were stains on the walls where rainwater entered in bad weather. There was a typing room but the machines were seized and useless. Brendan's office was intact, although as a bankrupt he could not use it any more. A border solicitor's office. Metal filing cabinets. A roll-top desk. A bookcase with law reports. There was a strongroom downstairs where deeds were kept. The word Solicitor picked out on the window glass in gold letters, the gilt flaking, pocked, everything shabby, gathering the texture of the years to it. The room that wills were read in, the room where deeds were witnessed. You didn't want this room to be too clean, the clients expected it to be worn, somehow troubled. There was a chair for the hollow-cheeked widows, the vindictive and the bereft, the upright and the underhand. There was a leather briefcase on the floor, scuffed leather with tarnished brass fittings with Brendan's initials picked out on it. He didn't bother with the briefcase any more. He didn't bother with any of it.

Bann died of pneumonia three weeks later in Daisy Hill Hospital and was to be buried on the last Sunday in February at a Presbyterian meeting house on the lake shore close to Lurgan. It was the first time they had been together since Brendan had left the mental hospital. They had early drinks in the golf club beside the metal bridge in Newry and drove thirty miles north to Lurgan. It was a day of low-cast cloud and biting rain driven across the flat dykelands and bents of the lough, the shore grasses blown flat, the lough water the colour of zinc. A tin sign nailed to a telegraph pole said that the *Wages of Sin Is Death*. They stopped short of the wake house and got out of the cars. From the open door they could hear women and men's voices raised in hymnal.

'We should go inside,' Jean said, but they stood by the cars and did not move. This was gospel country and they were unknown to it and it to them.

'Fucking Bann dragging us out here, we'll catch our deaths,' Hutchie said. No one answered. The rain, now mixed with sleet blew in across the lake. A cortège formed outside the house, men in dark suits and ties shouldered Bann's coffin and the pastor walked in front of them in neckcloth and robe, his book in his hand. The women did not join the cortège but you could hear their voices uplifted in song from the house. The coffin passed the Bureau people and none of the cortège looked up. The Bureau people fell in behind the last of the funeral and followed it two hundred yards to a small graveyard on a rise beside the lake. Brendan was drenched but walked on and the rest followed. Brendan stopped at the cemetery gate and the others stopped with him. The grave had already been opened, wet clay in a mound beside it. The coffin was lowered and four men passed canvas straps under it and readied it to be lowered into the earth. The minister stood at the head of the grave and opened his book. Foam blown from the lake surface formed spume lines on the heap of clay. Sleet and rain driven horizontally blew the minister's robe into unbidden shapes and rifled the pages of his book. At the end he folded his book under his arm and turned to his congregants and said, 'Men, will ye be saved or will ye be damned?'

If he had been aware of the border people, the windlashed wretches by the cemetery gate, he had given no indication until at last he brought his gaze to bear on their ragged band.

'Will you be joined to the right hand of the risen Lord or will ye be cast down for all eternity?' In that moment they wished themselves better than they were and possessed of at least some vestige of the pilgrim heart.

The minister turned away from them and the wind carried his words across the torn surface of the lake and the wind blasted his wet soutane.

'That's Bann accounted for,' Hutchie said. 'There'll be no Captain Morgan's where he's going.'

Nora took Lorraine by the elbow and led her back to the car. When she looked back the minister stood upon the dug earth, one arm upraised and the wind pulled at his sleeve and vestments, animate effigy of his office. Owen wanted to stay to see Bann lowered into the ground but the others had had enough.

'What would you answer to the preacher's query,' Hutchie said, 'with Bann?'

'What query?'

'Would he be saved or would he be damned?'

'In the circumstances,' Nora said, 'that's a vulgar question.'

'I'm only just saying,' Hutchie said.

'Well maybe you shouldn't say it,' Jean said. 'Bann was a decent man, unlike some others you could name around here.'

Twenty-Eight

For a girl like Jean Brendan was low on cash and high on risk
and it was time to jump ship. Jean told everyone that the arc of
their love had been completed but she had wanted more from
Brendan, you always thought there was more. Fuck these men
who bore disappointment to their women like weary alms. They
treated them like they treated their business. It was always a consignment and it was always a double-cross. They wouldn't know
straight if it jumped up and bit them, Jean said. There always
had to be an angle, there always had to be a lie and Lorraine
was starting to see all hearts as contraband in the borderlands,
all that you are traded away by men with death in their faces.

Brendan was still gambling in a small way but his bets had
taken a strange turn and he wanted others to bet on the chances
of him dying in his sleep or alternatively of wasting away

with a disease. Hutchie would have pointed out the obvious to Brendan's face that there was no way to collect the winning bet if he was dead but none of the others in the Bureau thought to do it. To lie to others was second nature and to lie to yourself equally so.

Jean had enough dismay of her own to be going on with and didn't have room for anyone else's. She didn't come into McCrink's any more. Lorraine heard that she was seen out at Lacey's nightclub, in the Roadhouse and at Bogart's in Newry.

Brendan was smoking sixty red Silk Cut a day. He had plans for the future. He would open a chain of Bureaus along the border. They would open close to barracks and isolated border police posts so that they would have security. There were ironies here that appealed to him.

Hutchie hadn't been seen around the Bureau since the kidnapping of Owen, and Jean thought he was gone for good but he had been plotting all along and they should have seen it. A new shopping centre was being built at the Buttercrane Quay in Newry and when it opened there was a Bureau de Change on the concourse managed by Hutchie. There was aluminium signage, glass frontage and a bank teller's counter in blond wood with a cash counting machine. It was not Brendan's original Bureau with its aging beauty board and perspex glass window scored and pocked where a lone robber had sledged the glass out of its metal frame and snatched several thousand sterling off the counter. Hutchie's Bureau had uniformed guards and metal shutters. Jean said it was the way of the world that the mouthy one-eyed fucking gaolbird transcended them all.

Brendan said that he hadn't pitched for the new business but Nora had seen the letter he had got back from the management company of the shopping centre to say that a bank account was required for the lease. Even if Brendan hadn't been bankrupt no bank along the border was going to allow him to open an account and without an account there could be no tenancy. Up to this he had used his wife's identity to open accounts but following the collapse of the Bureau she had also been bankrupted.

Jean thought Brendan might ask her to open a bank account for him but they both knew that she would steal money that was not her own from such an account. What they had between them they had embezzled from others, their nights together were always tainted. No one trusted them any more and they had never trusted each other. It was what the lost cherished. Brendan drank in McCrink's every night where the clientele were already dead to themselves, their elegies long written in the heartbreak of their wives and children and their own brokenness.

Things were changing along the border. There were new frauds, contraband and drugs moving from the continent, and Brendan was in no position to take advantage. The market

traders and shop owners moved to Hutchie's Bureau. Hutchie
bought a house on Windsor Hill and was seen about the town
in an E-Class Mercedes but like Jean said there was a stink to
him that they were well rid of. There were those like Dominic
who when they went to prison came back honed as if by the
sound of metal gates closing. The high-walled yards and long
enclosed vistas were matters of the spirit, but a moral rot hung
about Hutchie.

Televisions and stereo equipment were sold from warehouses
on back roads. There was agricultural fraud with animals brought
across the border, smuggled back that night then re-sent with a
new claim for subsidy. Full containers of illegal cigarettes came
through the ports of Greenore and Dublin and Warrenpoint.
Galvanized sheds sold banned fireworks, bootleg vodka and
cigarettes, as though some debased revel was to be held. One
new trade held sway, transcendent in its rottenness. Lorraine
said she wanted nothing to do with it but it wanted something
to do with her.

Corrigan took Paddy to the docks in Dundalk. The channel
was muddy and shallow and required regular dredging and the
bigger boats had moved to more modern ports, but coal still
came in and scrap metal was exported.

'Bring the woman too,' Corrigan said. 'About time she had
her eyes opened.' Lorraine didn't say anything but she'd had

her eyes opened for a long time, she'd been watching them all at work and at play.

A container had been left on waste ground at the back of the port, the doors lay open and a wind off the marshes swayed them back and forwards, the rusted hinges groaning. It had always been a smuggler's coast, consignments coming in from freighters moored offshore, moody night scenes, grim-faced men with collars turned up against the cold and damp.

'I don't like this,' Lorraine said. The air from the salt-blasted marshes smelt of rotted kelp and of the dragging muds and islets dense with seabirds and guano.

'There's nothing to like about it,' Corrigan said, 'but it's what my job is about.'

'Hark at the big policeman,' Lorraine said. Corrigan gave her a look which said that he'd sicken her yet.

'You can keep your diesel and cigarettes and fucking little frauds. Smuggling people is where it's at now. People and drugs.' He wrenched open the left-hand door of the container and Lorraine winced at the barbarous grind of metal on metal.

'Twenty-eight Chinese freighted in at four grand a piece. You get them here, they disappear, you never see them again. Not my kind of business but somebody's business.'

'Not your kind of business my eye,' Lorraine said. 'Where are the people?' There were water bottles and discarded and soiled clothing on the floor on top of flattened cardboard boxes.

There were sleeping bags and food wrappers and a bucket in the corner to act as a toilet. Lorraine said it in a whisper but the walls of the freezer unit magnified her words.

'Where are the people?'

Corrigan stepped inside the container and his shoe touched a cassette deck which lay on its side. An eerie and slowed-down gavotte began to play. A girl singing in Chinese in some long-ago wharfside bar, her voice fading as the cassette batteries ran flat.

'This is the future,' he said. 'Fuck the border and the fucking Bureau. The whole world's a Bureau now.'

But there was still a border. The authorities referred to some roads as *concession* and other roads as *unapproved*. As though these passages from one place to the next, from light to darkness, derived their authority from being approved or from what might be conceded to them. A man parks a diesel tanker on an unseen causeway which runs across the bog at Carrickcarnon. Cars drive along the causeway and he steps across the stream marking the border and fills the tank with diesel on which duty has not been paid. This is criminal behaviour and if you told him so he would laugh in your face. His world is not your world, perfidy in the grain of the place.

Twenty-Nine

Speedy was more often in the news than out of it. He had been shot at in Belfast but had survived because he was wearing a Kevlar vest. Paddy didn't like guns or any violence more than necessary. He didn't like the attention that they brought but also said he knew there were people out there a whole lot better at guns than he was and he didn't want to give them any excuse to show what they knew. Speedy was flamboyant. He was photographed taking cocaine in the back of a limousine. When the photograph appeared in the press he put a twenty thousand pound bounty on the head of the man he believed to have taken it. He liked to be in the news and he liked to taunt people.

'Paddy needs to get away from that buck Speedy,' Jean said, 'for he'll not last another year.'

Sunday afternoon drinking. There'd been a sulky race on

the dual carriageway that morning and the winner had been disputed so they'd come back to the Hermitage to watch video of the finish. Speedy maintained that he was the fittest one there. He said he'd take on any man in the bar in a foot race up Canal Street. He said he knew the peelers were after him. He said he knew the paramilitaries were after him. Three months earlier he'd walked up to the editor of the *Sunday World* who had been covering Fegan's activities for eighteen months and threatened him. If he wanted to get killed he was going the right way about it. The dealer who had shot Speedy phoned McDowell afterwards and said to *tell Speedy next time he won't be so lucky. I'll get it right* and he did get it right.

There had been several large drug seizures on both sides of the border, including an £800,000 consignment seized at Balbriggan which was thought to have come in by sea.

It was early May. Because it was Sunday the streets were empty. There were poplar trees outside the courthouse and the canal was overhung by cherry trees, drifts of fallen blossom on the water, formal and still in the afternoon.

Two men came into the bar. They were wearing false moustaches and wigs and both were carrying an automatic pistol in their right hand. It was said afterwards that Speedy lifted a bar stool and tried to fight them off with it. As Speedy was known to wear a bulletproof vest they knocked him to the ground and shot him seventeen times in the face and skull. A report in the

Guardian newspaper said that Speedy's brains were 'spread all over the floor'. On post-mortem it was found that Speedy still had three bullets in his arm and shoulder from the previous attempt. Seconds before he was shot Speedy was reported to have said It's the Provies, it's the Provies indicating that the gunmen were members of the provisional IRA. There is no way of knowing who they were. Of the seventy possible witnesses in the bar at the time, none made themselves available for interview. Reports of Speedy's last words cannot be considered reliable. They may have been inaccurately reported or they may have been invented in an attempt to deflect blame. Dominic and Mary had both asked for mercy. Most people did and if it was truly reported that Speedy wished to identify his killers rather than plead for his life it seems anomalous unless he knew that his life was forfeit from the start. When it came to dying Speedy was almost the last of them and he'd hardly got started.

Thirty

Lorraine told Jean that Paddy was going to move out of Newry and go to Florida to live what Lorraine called a sophisticated life. She knew in her heart that Paddy was leaving her. Jean told her to wise up that Paddy was attached to this unwholesome place like a child to the tit but Lorraine was convinced. Jean had seen Paddy on the steps of the courthouse in Trevor Hill two days beforehand. He was with a barrister in a wig and had his attaché case by his side. Another man came down the steps with his solicitor and tried to put his head down and walk past Paddy, but Paddy called out to him and when he lifted his head Paddy gobbed full in his face and left him there with spit running off his chin. It didn't look much like a man who was looking for a sophisticated life to Jean but she daren't tell it, you never knew which way Lorraine was going to jump these days.

Still, Lorraine had thought that week that Paddy was trying to finish with her. He was standing in her flat looking out the window, over his shoulder she could see the Enterprise running along the nighttime skyline, its windows lit, and she wondered did the words cross his mind as they did hers. *All aboard.*

He said he was getting involved in some dangerous business as if his business was not always dangerous. She thought it was an excuse. Did he not understand that death was no impediment to her? That she had imagined their bullet-riddled bodies sprawled in marginal land at the edge of town, hapless and betrayed? These things did not concern her but she had glimpsed brochures in his briefcase. There were burnished seas and palm trees, light coming back at you from angular white buildings. She saw him lost to her in Florida and to himself, shading his eyes against the light of endless seas, misplaced in the world. He would be vulnerable to American things, to the prairie expanses, the great reach of continent.

Two days later an envelope was pushed under her door. These things happened in Newry, where people spoke as if each sentence had evidential value. There were poison pen letters, people were named in graffiti as touts and abusers, there was always a corrosive undertow. The envelope contained a cutting from the *Sunday World* newspaper.

Money laundering through Bureaus de Change is nothing new for Irish gangsters.

The first Bureau de Change was set up in Newry in the early eighties by disbarred solicitor Brendan McNamee.

He had been in banking before becoming a top criminal lawyer.

He set up the first bureau after being struck off as a lawyer for dipping into his clients' accounts.

McNamee laundered money for most border smugglers but he fell foul of a cartel of North Louth diesel smugglers who kidnapped his son.

His business attracted the attention of Paddy Farrell, the criminal mastermind based in Newry and first exposed by the Sunday World.

'Kind of covers the whole thing,' Jean said.

'I suppose,' Lorraine said.

'Is Paddy that thing?'

'What?'

'A criminal mastermind.'

'How would I know?'

'If you don't know, then who does?'

Lorraine didn't answer.

'You any idea who sent it? Hutchie maybe? Corrigan?'

'It makes no difference to me.' She was telling the truth. She would not be intimidated. Lorraine was all high stakes, and only Mary McGlinchey had seen it.

The Bureau was closed more often than it was open. Jean called to Lorraine's flat once a week and they drank Bacardi and talked about what already seemed like days gone by. Hutchie had used that word *bogey* meaning bogus. He used it about forged bank drafts and stolen cars and those intent on wrongdoing, but Lorraine said she knew the uses of the word better now. Men were bogey but so was aloneness. Love was bogey. Jean knew that Lorraine was religious and asked was God in his Commandments and his son dead on the cross bogey also but Lorraine did not answer. She did not seem herself and used some coarse phrases.

'Some women like that dirty talk,' Jean said, 'but she come to the wrong house if she thought it was acceptable in my company.'

The flat wasn't clean which was not like Lorraine. The surfaces were dirty and there were dishes in the sink, dead bluebottles on the windowsill. The fridge was empty save for a carton of milk gone rancid. Jean did not think it her place to say anything though Lorraine sat in front of an unlit fire wearing a fine cotton blouse you could spit through and thin leggings like a pallid child of legend.

'There's not a pick on her,' Jean said to Nora. 'A gust of wind and she'd be blew clean away and we'd never see her back.'

Lorraine said that when the children of the pharaohs died

their bodies were embalmed and they were placed in their tombs, with food and their favourite toys, where they would wait for their journey to the houses of the dead. Jean said that Lorraine scared her when she talked about the houses of the dead. Lorraine's Peugeot 307 sat in Soho car park under the plane trees, the paintwork eaten into by the rainborne grime of the town.

She cooked for him but Paddy had no interest in food. 'There's only one thing you're interested in,' she said, but she wondered if he was even interested in that any more. When he came to bed she lay still under him, her body like an empty house broken into.

In an effort to make things better in the bedroom, as Jean said, for Lorraine and Paddy, Jean brought a book called *The Joy of Sex*, a manual by Dr Alex Comfort. She didn't know that you could be a doctor of sex. Jean found it in the boot of Brendan's car and gave it to Lorraine. It said on the cover that it was a gourmet guide to lovemaking, whatever the fuck that is, Jean said. There were line drawings of a bearded man and a woman who did not shave under her arms having sex in well-lit places with cushions.

At the start Lorraine had loved the flat. She made it homely with fitted sheets and curtains from Corry's and all the little comforts that any woman would have in a home. She liked being in the flat in the daytime when everyone else has gone to work, the curtains moving in the breeze, barely heard voices from outside, the heart withheld in these set-apart places, the sunlit days gone adrift outside. But the days and weeks carried her further and further from memory. She wanted to curl up in pyjamas on the sofa with Paddy and watch the kind of films that made you weep and then you could turn your tear-stained face up to him but she remembered only the cold lost house in the mountains where she met Dominic and Mary.

The summer town settled into a memory of itself, the streets heat-struck and desolate. She spent a lot of time in her bedroom. She watched soaps on television with the sound turned down wondering who these silent people were and if they were refugees from cities that were dreamed of but never built. You could hear the Enterprise on the high bridge, hear the desolate railway yard hooters, carnival music from the Showgrounds where the funfair was. From her back window, the houses on the hillside looking rickety, dust-blown. She believed the town to have some kind of wraith life, suited old men and women in black occupied the benches on Hill Street.

At nightfall she would leave the flat to go to the Dominican church where she would kneel in the near-dark, solitary candles flickering and the black friars about the work of the soul half-hidden behind the altar and vestry. The candles will blaze up for vespers but for now it is quiet. Lorraine kneels facing the altar and thinks she sees movement in the other pews, that there are other veiled and forgotten women at prayer. She bows her head. *Now I lay me down to sleep I pray my Lord my soul to keep.*

Lorraine started to let things slide in the weeks before her death. She went back over what had happened between Paddy and herself, the border runs, the carriage at Giles Quay, the runs to England, the shadowy tradecraft of disappointed lovers, walking the spied-on streets of what you thought you were. The lover that you had been trailed, shadowed, the left-behind artefacts of your being picked over for broken promises. You know from the start that you would not love as you should.

Jean helped her pack up the flat, everything she owned put into the Peugeot, and she drove back to Drogheda. On her way she stopped at the caravan. She found the train driver's cap wrapped in the sheets. The brass badge had turned green and there was mildew on the brim and in the cloth interior. She placed it on the metal locker beside the bed and put her head down on the pillow.

She sat down on the bed and placed her hand on the damp sheets and thought of a night with Paddy beside her and the carriage creaking with their movement when there was a bang on the door and a youth's voice shouted, *Any chance of a ride in the train for me, missus?* Paddy got out of the bed and went to his case. He took out the taser and went naked to the door. She could hear the teenager's laughter as they ran away. *Leave them* be, *Paddy*, she spoke softly from the bed, *they're only youngsters*. Paddy opened the door and stood looking out into the darkness. She had never looked at him like this before. The whiteness of his skin standing looking out into the rain, bare to the whole world, the deep hollow at the base of his spine, his legs planted. What was naked in a man. *Choo choo missus* the teenagers called out laughing as they ran down the dunes. *Choo fucking choo*.

Thirty-One

Witnesses said that Lorraine knew guns, though no one was able to say how she came by this knowledge. Two weeks before the events of 12th May she approached the wife of gun dealer Leo Murray who had advertised a shotgun for sale. Later when she examined the gun Leo Murray said that she 'gave the impression' that she was used to guns. Lorraine called at the house and examined the weapon. 'She seemed to be a girl used to handling guns. She knew how to open and examine the weapon and gave me the impression that she'd been clay pigeon shooting in the past. She seemed to know all about guns.' She did not buy the shotgun from Murray then.

None of the Bureau people touched firearms. Paddy carried a taser in his attaché case. At his inquest it was said that the taser could give a shock of 30,000 volts, enough to stun a grown man and leave him shaken and confused for a period of time. But police were unable to prove if the unlicensed weapon had ever been used. In fact Paddy had never used it and it was found in the corner of Lorraine's bedroom covered in dust and uncharged. In the end it was about what you could get away with. For the ordinary person caught in wrongdoing the game is over. For the Bureau crew being caught was only the start of the game and a conviction was a long way down the track if it happened at all. In the meantime there were statements to be quashed, witnesses to be undermined, evidence to be tested, juries to be tampered with. You'd be surprised what a court will swallow, Paddy said, but if you were caught a gun was a guarantee of prison time. Following a robbery attempt Hutchie brought a pickaxe handle into the Bureau but Nora just looked at it and said what am I supposed to do with that, and they all looked ashamed and the pickaxe handle was left up against the wall in the back office.

'I never knew you had to pay for a grave,' Lorraine said, as if one was alloted to you the day you were born and this followed you through your life until it fell to you to need it. But it wasn't so. It had to be paid for and there was nothing in this life or hereafter that could not be bought and sold. She asked the gravedigger in St Peter's cemetery how you would go about buying one and he sent her to her neighbour, the undertaker

Patrick Townley. Townley said afterwards that he was surprised that a young woman with her whole life in front of her would buy a grave but people did things like that.

'People don't be buying the one grave,' the gravedigger said to Lorraine. 'You're as well going for the double.'

'One's a bit lonely-sounding I suppose.'

'They're cheaper by the pair as well but it makes no odds,' the man said. 'Anyhow who'd be buying a single grave?'

The gravedigger said that digging graves was only part of the job. You had to cut the grass and spray the gravel paths. You'd be surprised how much work was in it. Artificial flowers long-faded blew off the graves and you were always picking something up or setting it right, a vase toppled and smashed or a long-extinguished eternal light in a scratched dome, all of death's trinketry A graveyard was never as still a place as you thought. Some people visited graves every day or every week but there was many's a grave was never visited, he said, nor never would be.

Paddy had patches of eczema on his arms and torso and it had started to appear on his face. Hutchie had put it down to exposure to solvents used to launder diesel and called him a scabby bastard behind his back. Jean said that if laundered diesel caused eczema then half of the people she knew would be clean rotten with it. But it hurt Lorraine to see him looking at her through a mask of affliction. She had read that eczema was often a symptom of anxiety. Nora said that she had suffered from it once and the worst part of it was the relentless itch and sleepless nights. Nora said that sunlight was good for eczema and dermatitis and Lorraine saw Paddy again standing on a Florida beach, caught in a healing light and free from care, and she could not bear it.

The gun dealer Murray said that he brought the gun to the house in Boyle O'Reilly Terrace on 7th September. There is no evidence that Lorraine paid him for it.

That week she took Paddy from Boyle O'Reilly Terrace down the Twenties to the gate of St Peter's cemetery. Jean said her interest in the dead was morbid but Lorraine didn't see it like that. The funerals passed the house in Boyle O'Reilly Terrace, often there was a horse-drawn hearse, she could hear the hooves in the funeral silence and over the wall the tossed black plumes. Her relatives were buried in the cemetery. And when you went to sleep at night the dead watched over you, were forever vigilant where others lost faith. The graves were well-tended with flowers in glass domes and eternal flames in lantern-shaped cases, but Paddy only had eyes for the cadaver graves along the church wall which had the hollow corpses of the dead rendered in stone on the mausoluem lid.

When they got to the door of the church Paddy said, 'I'm not going near thon thing inside.'

'It's just history,' Lorraine said.

She had not thought that Paddy was given to black imaginings but it was the only time she saw anything close to fear in his eyes. She did not press him and when she said on the way back that the door of the Newgate death cell where the saint had been held was on show in the church he said he had seen enough of prison doors and didn't intend to set eyes on another one in all his born days. He drove back to Newry that evening and she did not hear from him for five days. She did not mention the saint again. And she did not tell him when she crossed the road to the undertaker Townley's house the day after they had gone to the church and bought a double grave in the cemetery for two hundred pounds.

The last time Jean had seen Lorraine they had a fight. Lorraine was in one of her Holy Joe moods which irritated Jean. It was all fucking benedictions and venerations, God coming at you in incense-wreathed elaborations. Jean had taken up with a man called Crozier from Richhill who was an elder in his church. Crozier drove a Transit and listened to gospel music on the radio and there was a backwoods feel to him and for all that Lorraine was Jean's friend Crozier considered her a papist and therefore apostate.

'If you make up your mind to be a nun you'd better be sure not to let the mother superior see Paddy Farrell climb over the convent walls.'

'At least Brendan used to take you to a hotel,' Lorraine said. Jean said nothing. Crozier drove her to disused flax dams and old water-filled quarries and got her to climb into the back of the van between the seats. Jean wondered why he picked these places. She could see her own water-logged corpse being taken from the still waters, limp and dredged.

'I hear you took Paddy back,' Jean said, although she knew that Lorraine had never let go of him.

'He has to be on his best behaviour,' Lorraine said. 'He's on his final warning.' She'd given Paddy another chance or she'd given herself another chance, she didn't really know which. When Paddy was away on business Lorraine would go down to Giles Quay and spend the night in the caravan on her own. Teenagers had written their names on the wood panelling. Sand had blown up against the side of it so that she could barely get the door open. Water had run from a leak in the tarred canvas roof and rotted the flooring at one end. She thought she had pulled up the bed the last time they had left but it was unmade, the sheets bunched showing the mattress underneath.

There were comics she had left there from when she was at school, *Judy* and *Bunty*, and she would lie on the bed reading by the light from the Tilley. She wanted Paddy to know what it was like to come here when you were young, she wondered if Paddy had ever been young, she could not find the words but if she did there would be something of boyhoods coming to an end, of girls backed up against walls, kissed under streetlights, working your way under clothing, zips and catches, the held warmth, the taking of what you were allowed, the giving away of something you had only just come to owning.

Thirty-Two

The cold came early that year, isobars packed all the way down from the north, hoar frosts on the grass in Boyle O'Reilly Terrace and in the Lourdes stadium. Even in early September the evenings felt dark, the weather bringing an end of days feel to it. Paddy was travelling to Dublin two or three times a week, stopping off at Boyle O'Reilly Terrace when he knew Peggy and Dessie were out, driving up the Twenties to the gardens, the maroon Mercedes standing on the narrow street.

If anyone was looking for Paddy they knew where to find him.

For those last months it felt as if they were their outlaw selves again and Paddy said it was better this way. Lorraine said that she liked them being lovers in flight with no one to depend on but themselves but she missed the flat and the feeling in your stomach when you heard Paddy's key in the door, and she missed the days and nights in the carriage at Giles Quay when she came to his bed and he to hers.

A month after she came back to the terrace Lorraine answered the door at number 36 Boyle O'Reilly Terrace, Corrigan standing on the front step.

'Is Paddy there?'

'You know right and well he's not. The car's not here.'

'Can I come in?' She didn't want him standing on her mother's doorstep and she didn't want him in the house.

'What are you here for? Is he in trouble?'

Corrigan was wearing a tan linen jacket with a blue shirt and a white tie. There was a blue satin handkerchief in his top pocket. He had on squarish dark glasses with a brown tint and she wondered why he wore them on a dull day.

'Man like Paddy, in trouble?'

'Well what do you want then?'

'I just wanted to see the love nest.' Dropping in a laugh that wasn't a laugh.

'This is my mother's house, if that's what you mean.'

Corrigan pushed past her. She didn't want him in the small hallway of the house with his smell of cologne and his policeman's way of making everything seem less than it was. He took off the glasses and looked around the hall, a forensic stare, everything weighed and found wanting. The photographs and ornaments, cherished way-posts of family on the hall table lifted and polished, all her sweet lifetimes already in jeopardy, looking tawdry and abandoned like crime scene effects.

He picked up a photograph of Lorraine taken when she was at school. The patent shoes. Pleated skirt to the knees. The way a child lets their arms hang by their sides. The badly trimmed fringe. The collared wool coat buttoned up to the chin and the white knee socks.

'I seen you the other morning. Out early.'

'I go out early every morning. I go to first mass every day.'

'Mass?' That flat policeman delivery again. Letting things hang in the air. 'Sign of a guilty conscience.'

'I've nothing to be guilty about. Unlike some people.' It didn't come out the way she wanted. It sounded like some wan thing you'd say in the playground, tears in the eyes, girl fists clenched. She wanted to ask him why he spent time with Brendan and Paddy and the rest, with him supposed to be a policeman, but this was the border, and law did not mean what it was supposed to mean. She knew that now.

'Tart little miss, aren't we? There's no such thing as innocence in this world, I'm afraid to say. We all got something to hide.' Lorraine trying not to think about the case on top of the wardrobe in her bedroom, the flimsy catalogue items crumpled and hidden, all of it seeming furtive and sinful.

'Did he take you to the apartment?'

'What apartment?'

'The new apartment he just bought in Dublin, he didn't say?'

'He doesn't have to tell me everything.' Lorraine bit her lip. She didn't care what Paddy did with his money. For all she knew, buying an apartment was a good move. She knew that Brendan had owned a hotel at one time but it had been burned down and Brendan had been given a large sum in compensation. This was said with sly looks which she took to mean that fraud had taken place, the hotel had been bought with the purpose of burning it down and collecting the insurance. If that was what Paddy was doing it suited her. It meant that he was more than ever involved in the border life, entrapped in his own doings. It was the other possibility that concerned her. That Paddy was settling down, transferring money into legitimate businesses. She didn't like the word mistress but she wasn't stupid. She would hate if anyone used the word mistress about her but at least there was a bit of swank to it. When it came down to it she understood that she was part of the illicit life and if Paddy reneged on that then he reneged on her.

'Don't worry, Lorraine, we'll look after you.'

'I don't need looking after. Not from the likes of you.'

'You'd be seeing to Paddy two or three times a week, would that be about accurate?'

'I see him.'

'That wasn't what I said.'

'I know what you said.'

'I know everything about you, miss.'

But there were things that Corrigan did not know about Lorraine. There were things that nobody knew. The missal on the hall table with her rosary beads and white satin gloves trimmed with lace on top and a shotgun borrowed and thoughts of sinning in the dark.

'He's playing with the big boys now. You'd think he'd be a bit worried. You'd think he'd wake up at night sweating. Does he?'

'Does he what?'

'Wake up in the middle of the night. I'm forgetting, he never stays the night, does he, heads back to Newry.'

'None of your business what he does.'

'He sold that flat of yours, didn't he? Putting a bit of cash together for Florida. Did he ever take you there, to Florida? The Sunshine State? Played a bit of golf there myself. Gave Paddy the brochures for the laugh. Never thought he would take to it the way he done.'

'I think you should go now.'

'That's the trouble, isn't it? You and me. We can't see ourselves settling down in Florida. All them reptiles and alligators and the like. We're homebirds. But Paddy isn't. He has the tickets bought. Wouldn't be surprised if he has some little local honeys there as well. Pretty little things, the Florida women. Snap your fingers and they're sitting in your lap.'

Lorraine knew what Corrigan was trying to do but she could not help seeing these women who walked in clear-skinned gravity on beaches warmed by the sun. They were not subject to the border frosts, and their sorrows if they had any were easily borne under clear skies.

There was a dream that she never told anyone even Jean that Paddy would retire from everything and come and live with her and they would grow old in Drogheda walking home together on smoky streets in the shadow of the great bridge, the grey riveted frame, the river almost unseen below. The dream always had a lamplit feel to it. They would be greeted by neighbours on homely streets, they would be frugal in all things and would have provided for everything in life. She told everyone that by the time she was thirty she wanted a gravestone and a grave picked out. Either people laughed at her or they turned away looking frightened, but nothing about death frightened her growing up beside the graveyard with undertakers and other practitioners of the grisly trades for neighbours and three or four times a week the funeral rites coming over the wall with sometimes the sound of a priest on a tannoy and sometimes a woman weeping.

*

She asked Paddy what he was doing in Dublin and was it true that he had a high-end apartment in Ballsbridge on the south side of Dublin? He said that he did but it was part of his business. He was able to pay cash for it and only a fool would turn a deal like that down. He was rumoured to have connections with gangland figures in Dublin including those associated with the murder of journalist Veronica Guerin. He is alleged to have double-crossed them by hijacking a consignment of cannabis when they were under police and media pressure following the shooting of Guerin. Other reports said that Speedy had cheated Paddy out of the same consignment. But all Lorraine wanted to know was did he bring anyone else to the Ballsbridge flat?

'No.'

'Then why don't you bring me?'

'It's rented out.'

'Is it a nice place?'

'It is.'

'Is it anything like the place you took me to in Larne?'

On his death the papers described Paddy as a drug dealer and Lorraine heard it said when people thought she was out of earshot. Lorraine did not think drugs were moral but Hutchie said that there was so much money to be made in drugs so why wouldn't he?

'Are you?'

'What?'

'Selling drugs?'

'Who told you that?'

'Doesn't matter.'

'Hutchie. I'd say it was that half-blind fucker.'

'Doesn't matter who it was. You still haven't answered me.'

'You think you're going to get an answer?'

'A girl can ask, can't she?'

Paddy was smiling although he wasn't looking at her.

Lorraine seeing the danger she had walked into and withdrawing into a certain girlishness, the lisped syllables, *a girl can ask*. There was no room for introspection in Paddy's work. You did what you did and consequences came your way or they did not. You didn't think about what was right and what was wrong and you didn't want those around you pointing out the morality or otherwise of your actions. If your work involved certain merchandise then that was your own hardhearted business and not for others to judge. Paddy walked out of the house and she didn't see him for two weeks.

Thirty-Three

The inquest into the death of Patrick Farrell was held in Drogheda Coroner's Court on 20th September. The coroner Dr Liam Millar concluded that the inquest of Lorraine Farrell could not be held on the same day as relatives were not present in court.

The bodies of Paddy and Lorraine had been taken to the morgue of the Lourdes hospital for autopsy the following day. It is not clear whether undertakers were employed or if they were taken by ambulance. The main hospital had been built in the 1950s. It is flat-roofed with limestone on the upper facade and brickwork below. There is a forty-foot-tall stylized crucifix inset on the brick facade of the hospital. The ancillary buildings reach across the site to Boyle O'Reilly Terrace. Functional structures which suggest that this is where the work is done, where laundry is washed in industrial machines, where medical waste is dealt with, the fluid and blood-soaked leavings, the bandaging and lints of the wards and theatres, the ragged bunting of the place incinerated. This is where you find the pathology labs, haematology and clerical services. This is where the dead are taken.

The undertaker Townley said in his deposition that Wilton was 'in a terrible state and shouting that there had been an accident'. Townley went up to the bedroom. He saw two bodies. The man was lying naked on the bed. He had severe head wounds which appeared to be on the right side. There was blood on the walls and on the floor. He then saw Lorraine's body in a crouched position on the floor. He checked for signs of life. She was stone cold and rigor mortis had set in. She was wearing only a bra. There was a shotgun on the floor.

The letter Wilton found in Lorraine's handbag was given to the court usher. The usher handed it to the coroner who read it and retained it. The contents of the letter were not disclosed to the inquest but it is believed that the letter contained instructions concerning Lorraine's funeral. The inquest was told that Lorraine Farrell had sent letters to her sister in London and had also written to Patrick Farrell's wife.

Pathologist Joseph Stuart, who carried out a post-mortem examination on Patrick Farrell, said that he had an extensive blast injury to the right side of his head which was blown away.

He estimated that the shotgun was discharged from a distance of less than three feet. He said it was virtually impossible for the injury to have been self-inflicted. He concluded that death was due to a cerebral injury consistent with a shotgun blast.

When contact range is measured in feet the entrance is a single round hole because the pellets penetrate the target as a single mass. Soot deposition is present. Searing reddish-brown rim or skin blistering. At a distance of more than three feet the shot starts to disperse. The wound shows serrated or crenellated edges referred to as the 'rathole effect'.

There was unhappiness that the autopsy was performed by a local pathologist rather than the state pathologist, family members feeling that there was something more to be learned from the physical evidence, that there were sequences of finding that were not rigorously adhered to, some truth in the scene before the investigators that was not yielded up. Perhaps they thought that the local pathologist would not have the experience of a state pathologist in dealing with violent crime. His practice more concerned with car accidents, drownings. Young men driving their cars into trees on remote country roads. Young women throwing themselves from the Boyne Bridge into the river below, drifting downstream into the reed beds, They thought that he may not have had access to crime lab facilities. Did he look to see if there was pinching of the interdigital groove between forefinger and thumb to see if the flesh was caught between the trigger and the trigger guard, indicating that the dead person in fact had fired a shot? Were there transfer stains or impact stains to give clues about the dynamic of the event? There's a vocabulary to these things. But there is no evidence that the pathologist was other than efficient and competent. It would not be unusual for the family to feel that they were owed something more from the proceedings but the primary purpose of an inquest is to identify the deceased and establish how, when and where death occurred. It is an inquisitorial process. It does not include a finding of liability, either civilly or criminally, on the part of any person. There's a half-told feel to the written accounts of the witnesses. There are eerie spaces.

The newspapers cast Lorraine as a *blonde beauty* and Paddy as a *millionaire gangster* and a *crime boss*. You learn from the papers that Lorraine had told her mother that Paddy was going to call to the house on Wednesday, 10th September. She had told her mother that she had bought a grave and seemed very happy about it. Dessie Wilton had also been told about the grave and also said that Lorraine was extremely happy about it but that he found it very morbid in a girl of her age.

Townley the undertaker said that he had shown Lorraine the grave beside her grandmother's grave and that she had paid him in cash.

Lorraine had inspected the shotgun at the gun dealer's

house and had told him she would give him two hundred pounds' deposit. He hadn't renewed the shot gun licence because he had planned to sell it. He said that he had intended to call down to Boyle O'Reilly Terrace to take the gun back on Tuesday, 9th September, the day before the shootings. He said he was tired and forgot about it and felt physically sick in his stomach when he heard that there had been a shooting at Boyle O'Reilly Terrace. He said he had not given Lorraine any cartridges.

A firearms certificate is required to purchase cartridges. Lorraine did not have a firearms licence. Where did the cartridges come from? Murray's first act when he heard about a shooting was to call the police. He did not say why he thought that the shooting might have involved the shotgun Lorraine had taken from him the previous day.

If Murray had acted on the Tuesday night, if he had not forgotten to call down for the shotgun, then the gun would have been taken out of the picture and there would have been no killing. But if he had agreed a price or at least a deposit then why was he calling down to take the gun back?

Gardai discovered a black PVC dress, white panties, Paddy's trousers and a taser in the bedroom. All the papers reported this and the fact that Lorraine was wearing only a bra. All the papers had the lingered-over details. Detective Garda Pat O'Neill said that Paddy was lying on the bed with his hands on his stomach and that Lorraine was behind the bed in a pool of blood. Her body was on top of the shotgun.

The post-mortem examination was carried out at Our Lady of Lourdes Hospital on 12th September, two days after the double shooting. Dr Joseph Stuart said that the shot had been fired from a distance of one to three feet and that it was not self-inflicted, that it would have been impossible for Paddy to have pulled the trigger. Lorraine however was able to pull the trigger when she shot herself so the pathologist must have come to his conclusion by examining Paddy's body position.

A substantial sum of money was found in Paddy's trousers. One thousand pounds sterling in ten pound notes was also found in the house. The *Irish Independent* reported that four shots had been fired, two of them had come from the direction of Lorraine's body and had been directed at the ceiling of the bedroom. Lorraine was characterized as a good daughter who regularly cleaned the house and went to mass every day. Although friends and family had been concerned that she had lost a stone and a half in weight in the months before she died.

You try to work out the sequence. *He's on the bed. She has put the mask on, put this on so I cannot see your eyes, my beloved.* What is she saying? *Something special for you. Something special my love. All aboard.* The shotgun has two tumblers, two hammers, two barrels. It has to work that way that she shoots him with the first barrel and kills him. Paddy wasn't the kind of man to let her take two shots. The noise of the gun in the small bedroom. Then she shoots herself. But she has fired four shots. One for Paddy, one for Lorraine, and two into the ceiling. Did she fire two shots before she killed herself? The gun slipping away. Or courage failing her. *I can't I can't O dear sweet Lord I can't.*

The inquest into the death of Lorraine Farrell was held the following April. Her death could have been dealt with at Paddy Farrell's inquest but no members of Lorraine's family attended that inquest and the coroner said that although a family solicitor was present no proceedings should go ahead in the absence of the deceased's family. Paddy Farrell's inquest had attracted national press coverage but Lorraine's inquest was low key. Cause of death was established as a wound to the head inflicted by a shotgun blast. The local papers said that Lorraine was friendly and popular. That she went to the gym three or four times a week, drove a car, the Peugeot 307, and was well dressed, although no one knew how she could afford her lifestyle. Suggestions that Lorraine and Paddy died as a result of a suicide pact were dismissed by police.

It was reported that Lorraine had several boyfriends before Paddy but that none of the relationships was serious. The *Drogheda Independent* said that she was depressed in the weeks leading up to her death. It said that unnamed neighbours heard raised voices during the day of the killings but that they did not connect the two events and that it was only in the following days that the significance of the raised voices was realized. You doubt if there had been the kind of argument that raised voices implied. A row with raised voices in a small suburban house feels squalid and unlikely, the sounds of a domestic spilling out into an early afternoon street, not a prelude to what took place in Boyle O'Reilly Terrace. Perhaps another day but not this day, the self laid open and plundered. This was not a row followed by make-up sex, a tearstained quickie on top of the bedcovers. This was planned in advance, ritualized.

The autopsy report stated that two empty shotgun cartridges were found on the bedroom floor. This means that Lorraine shot Paddy then for some reason fired two shots into the bedroom ceiling and then shot herself. The purpose of the shots into the ceiling could not be ascertained unless the gun slipped twice as Lorraine sought to position it to shoot herself. The autopsy stated that Paddy could not have shot himself, positioned as he was on the bed. Lorraine, crouched on the floor was able to direct a shot at herself.

Theories were advanced as to Lorraine's state of mind. Spousal amorous jealousy is identified as the predominant type of murder-suicide. It typically occurs when an adult male, motivated by real or perceived termination of a romantic relationship, kills his spouse or consort and occasionally her new romantic interest. Studies have tried to ascertain whether murder-suicide is an outworking of a murderous intent or a suicidal intent. The Perversion of Virtue theory states that the primary impulse is to die by suicide. That the impulse to murder is secondary to the impulse to take your own life. By this account Lorraine decided to take her own life and then to kill Paddy as an impulse derived from a perversion of virtue, a loving intent perhaps. That he could not live without her. That his life and doings would collapse around him if he did not accompany her into the night. In murder-suicides with female perpetrators the majority of cases involve mothers killing their children and then taking their own lives. The mother decides to take her own life and decides in her distress that her children will not make it through life without her and takes them with her. But Paddy was not a child. In her distress and mortal jeopardy, did Lorraine see him as such and decide that he could not live without her? It feels unlikely. There is nothing in the textbooks, no case that comes close to the events in Boyle O'Reilly Terrace.

Senior police officers met in Drogheda. They dismissed the idea of a suicide pact and came to the conclusion that in the absence of any evidence to the contrary, the shootings would be treated as a murder-suicide. The number of cartridges initially indicated that Paddy had been shot twice but there is no suggestion that Lorraine missed the first shot. Paddy was on the bed. He hadn't moved. If he had been killed by the first shot, then why discharge a second?

You start to place other people in the room. Shadowy figures. This was the era of shadows. This was the time when people disappeared without warning. This was the time of unexplained shootings, of clandestine alliances, zones of subterfuge, zones of dread. This was the border. There were set-ups, double-crosses, betrayal. Subterfuge was the currency, the game seen far into the future, the deep tradecraft.

Thirty-Four

Corrigan walked with a limp. He had been abducted from the Boyne Valley Hotel and had been held and beaten for two days by the IRA over a missing consignment of vodka which he had undertaken to sell on their behalf. He was a creature of the ill-lit environs of border hotels, hanging around them in a vagrancy of his own making, part of him seemed to be lonesome for his old cohort and part of him was afraid they would come to him as ghosts. Their faces rose up in front of him. They're the aftermath of themselves, pale, trafficked across hidden borders.

Owen kept running into Corrigan. Corrigan would stop him on the street, put a hand on his chest, pin him against the wall.

'You're a law student, right? What was your da doing putting you in a car with Paddy Farrell? If you got stopped with Farrell and they recognized him you'd have ended up in the same prison cell, that's where you would have ended up, Mr Justice Gaolbird, and where would your legal career have been then? Not that maybe you have one coming, your da being Mr Brendan McNamee, legal adviser to the dregs of the border,' Corrigan said. Unseen hands are at work. Arcane trades are practised. You don't know what the agendas are but everything moves deathward. You can lose your life for good reason or you can lose it for nothing at all. Murders are staged, attributed to others. The named dead are abroad in the border night. Dominic, Speedy, Eamon, Carney. No one knows for certain who killed any of them and why. Ambiguity and deceit are second nature. Lorraine bought two graves. She borrowed a shotgun and wrote letters to her family which were not released by the coroner. The verdict of the Coroner's Court that she shot Paddy in the head and then shot herself is reasonable. Other aspects of proof are insubstantial, your thoughts drift away from the bedroom, the blood spatter and bone fragments. Lorraine *not herself* in the weeks leading up to the shooting.

The day following the death of Lorraine and Paddy a Ford Escort containing a crude pipe bomb was left outside Lorraine's family taxi business in Drogheda. The car had been stolen earlier that day in Newry, thirty-six miles away, and fitted with false number plates. The bomb exploded but did little damage. Police were unable to say who planted the car bomb or the purpose of it. The *Drogheda Independent* reported speculation that it might be something to do with the missing money. But it takes some time to organize a bomb run. When was it known that the money was missing? Was the disappearance of Paddy's money made public knowledge in time to enable a crude bomb to be constructed or sourced, for a car to be stolen and for a route to be planned to cross a fortified border without being apprehended? Did anyone know to look for the missing attaché case and the money in the immediate aftermath of the shooting? And if it was looked for and found to be missing, then this knowledge would only have been available to senior police officers. Or was the bomb run planned before Lorraine and Paddy's death for some unknown reason? In which case there is a chain of events of which we know nothing, the real story subterranean as are many border stories of that time, the truth fragile, allusive, not what you think it is.

Corrigan's in the Imperial. It's the evening after Lorraine's inquest and Owen has come at his request. He's hunched over a table. The Imperial isn't what it was, the smoked-glass windows are dingy and there's a crack in one which has been covered by tape. The velour banquettes are worn and the carpet sticks to your feet. Corrigan isn't the same man either. The border breaks you down, leaves you unnerved, glancing over your shoulder. Corrigan had been prosecuted for obtaining money by false pretences but the prosecution had not succeeded. Evidence had emerged that his car had been seen by customs officers acting as a scout car for fuel smugglers in the border region. He can hardly feel his legs since the beating. He was held for two days but he refuses to say where he was held and who was doing the holding. He says he doesn't know. The whole thing was a misunderstanding. He's been pushed to the margins, he says, all bets are off. He hasn't been feeling well this past few months. He hasn't crossed the border in years. He's been questioned in Dundalk about allegations that he's been a mole in the police, feeding information to paramilitaries and smugglers and he's afraid that if he crosses the border into the North he will be arrested and he will never come back.

Paddy and Lorraine. Nobody heard the shots, he says, not one soul. Boyle O'Reilly Terrace is a quiet place. Strange, he says, but never mind. Then there's the cartridges. Lorraine had a bag of cartridges but the dealer says he didn't give them to her, so who did? And Paddy's just lying there, she gets to lift the gun and fire at his head, Paddy lets her kill him, is that the way it happens? How many shots were fired? What happened to Paddy's briefcase, his clothing, his money? There are shadowy figures. There are plotters. How can there be so much death on this frontier? Don't ever believe the first thing you hear, Corrigan says, nor the second. He's doing the forensics in his head, he's breaking down the coroner's verdict. Lorraine bought a grave in the weeks before her death but what does that mean?

I bought a grave for myself thirty years ago and I'm only lucky that I didn't get to use it yet. Lorraine sent a note to her sister telling her what she wanted done when she died, but the sister didn't think it was a suicide note. It was just Lorraine. It was just the way she was. Forever talking about kings in tombs and dead saints and the like. Something doesn't feel right about it, he says, but then nothing feels right in this place of shadows we have made for ourselves. We didn't mean any harm, we only wanted to make a bit of money and have a good time, are you following me? It doesn't seem as if Corrigan can follow his own train of thought. He's going off on tangents. He says it stands by Lorraine that she knew to kneel in prayer though perhaps to the wrong god.

Owen asks him about the border run in the BMW when the police chased them but were left in their wake. Did Corrigan talk to the officers involved, persuade or bribe them not to pursue charges? Corrigan looks at him.

'They were chasing you, were they?'

'I was in the car. I saw them.'

'For fuck's sake. They weren't chasing you. They were an escort. Paid off. Both sides of the border. Brendan got me to set it up. They were protecting your da and his cash.'

'From who?'

Corrigan just looks at him. McKevitt. The McGlincheys. There was no shortage of suspects.

Owen knew that Brendan counted policemen among his acquaintances. Owen had been called to the barracks in Newry to take Brendan home drunk from the CID Christmas party. He'd driven his father to heavily defended border posts and waited outside for Brendan to leave by a side door and knew that if he had asked why his father was there he would not be told. *If you fly with the crows you get shot.* But he would not have asked. He did not want to know any more of what took place among these men, what they told and what they withheld, these figures who always seemed to have their faces turned from the light, these night cadres.

Corrigan looks around the bar. He knows nobody in the Imperial where once he knew everyone but there's a group of young men at the counter and he can tell those will be the new princelings of misrule, coming in from the borderlands, the strut and brag of them.

He tells Owen that he knew nothing then and he knows nothing now. If that wasn't true then what else was true?

'Did you arrange that police protection? Did Brendan pay you for it?'

'Son you don't know and you'll never fucking know so let me be. Do you remember McGlinchey?'

'Why would I forget him?'

'You mind when he was shot down in the street and when the uniforms arrived the son was going through his pockets.

The man's near dying or dead and the son has his hand in his pocket. He says the father told him to do it but what father would tell that to his son?'

It didn't feel strange to Owen. The son takes from the father what is willed to him and steals the rest, love requires that you kneel in his spilled blood and rifle pockets.

He wanted to say that his father had been brought up in a draper's shop on Monaghan Street in Newry and that Brendan had stood with his own father selling silk stockings to mill girls at the tram stop at the bottom of the street, running the material through his fingers, speaking of its qualities, the silken hose, how it fit the ankle, the calf, the thigh. He had done service to longing. He had done service to desire. If you could keep fathers to such memories. If you could thereby contain them. Brendan died that January. His body was light enough that cancer floated it away in weeks, besides his soul was a husk.

It's the early days of the Bureau. Owen and Brendan are driving home late, crossing the border. They reach the frontier at 2.30 a.m. Seven or eight articulated lorries were stopped on the plaza where the customs post had stood and across both lanes of the road. The lorries had been set on fire and were burning steadily. The spaces between the lorries looked black, geometric, deliberated over. Brendan moved the car slowly forward. Whatever had taken place here was over but the next thing might happen.

The smells of spilled fuel, heated metal, tar melt. To either side of them the unpeopled fields, the undrained fenlands, the burned trucks flaring. The expectation was abstract. There was an end place. In the morning there would be the burned-out frames. Owen quiet in the passenger seat. You could feel the heat through the glass of the passenger window. What does it mean, his father's face lit by fire in the night? Decades later someone asked the question, *Do you realize how many people around your father died violent deaths?* He said then that those were just the times. But he knew that it was not just the times. What he couldn't say was where all this death came from. If one father brought it in his wake, did all fathers dwell in blood and flame?

Thirty-Five

Paddy was wearing a black eyemask when he was shot. You
could see Lorraine ordering it from a catalogue, a mail order
kink feel to it. It went with the PVC dress. You wonder if she
put it on him? Fitting the straps around his head. *The man
she loved before all others.* Smoothing the fabric down over
his eyes. *No peeking.* She'd met him at the front door and led
him up the stairs, a corseted silent being. She'd gone on a
hen night in a saucy maid's uniform that made all her friends
laugh but now she did not recognize herself in the mirror, it
was not her body, this black-clad and fetishized thing. It was
a long way from Paddy naked wearing a train driver's cap
and his whispered words, *All aboard.* She told him he could
have whatever he wanted whenever he wanted, but there
were still concert tickets Blu-tacked to the wall above her

bed, pink hair clips, a ra-ra skirt with tassels hanging from the wardrobe door.

The man on the bed, naked, unseeing. Where did she hide the gun? If it was in the wardrobe he would hear the click of the latch, the hinges, the groan and squeak of its opening. Under the bed, pushing it into the darkness because Paddy's eyes as he came up the stairs would be aligned with the space under the bed. She's getting down on her knees. She'd be close to him, her head level with the bed, almost touching his leg, the skin, the little brownish hairs, and underneath it the man reek of him, the rank part of him, the musked flesh underneath the cologne he wore. The dress tight around her hips and thighs and the PVC gripping her skin, it was hard to get down, to reach under the bed and take out the shotgun so that it didn't catch on any of the things that are kept under beds, the discards, old trainers, worn-out luggage. Was it then she took the dress off? Did the barrel touch the metal bedframe? The gun feeling too big in the small room, the wooden stock, the hammer, the chased metal, the odour of graphite lubricant and powder residues. These elaborations of death, the little chasings, the fine-tooled metal, the graven death flowers. Paddy had to be attuned to the sound that a gun barrel might make against a bedframe or busted hair straightener or cup or glass, he'd recognize the sound of fine-grained barrelling and how it would ring out the peril that he found himself in. Enough to have him lift the mask and look to see his lover getting ready to place the muzzle against his temple, the barrel swaying as she tried to level the gun, more weight to it than she remembered, a slight blonde girl naked and ordinary in the moment, shoulder flesh pinched in the black bra strap. Absorbed in the mechanics of making it work. Thinking about what promises were, not this black thing in her bedroom. Your feet shoulder-width apart. Your knees neither stiff nor bent. How close to bring the barrel to his head. Knowing that she was naked and thinking that she should go and get dressed before she did this. Talking softly to him. *Wait. Don't look.* Paddy hearing death in her voice and mistaking it for another kind of promise, another kind of sinning. *All aboard.*

Thirty-Six

This is the border. The fields haunted, seen in wavering night-vision. The after-dark things astir, frontier rustlings, small beasts hunting in the drains and fir plantations. Something always at the periphery of your vision. These are the stalking times. From the Flagstaff you can see the lights of Newry down below and in the distance the flare on the underside of clouds that is Dundalk. You can look all the way down the lough to the Haulbowline lighthouse and the ships waiting outside the bar at the entrance to the lough, the sweep of the beam, and then to the south the lights on the television mast on Ravensdale mountain, to the north the gantry lights on the dock cranes at Warrenpoint, the night all in points of light, the night all in starred kindred.

*

Jean visited Lorraine's grave in January. She bought carnations in a garage, they were shopworn and jaded and she thought flowers would have been better left to Nora, but Nora has retired into herself and does not drive any more. She walks the precincts of her garden, sun-hatted, adrift in light and shade. From the graveyard you can see the high floodlights of Lourdes stadium and St Peter's with its gable Madonna where first the body of Dominic and then the bodies of Paddy and Lorraine were brought. Lorraine was laid in one grave but the other grave in the plot was empty. Paddy was buried in Newry twenty miles away in the graveyard attached to the Chapel of the Sacred Heart on the south side of town, the border side, at the point where the Enterprise emerges from the border cutting. From the Sacred Heart graveyard you can hear the Enterprise crossing the road south on the iron bridge.

Jean went into the church. Lorraine had talked about the saint's head but she had never seen it. Mass was being said in a side chapel. You could lose yourself in the high apses, the swung ballast of the chasuble trailing incense. She stood before the saint, the head collapsed inward with wisdom, the wrinkles and lobes, the eyes in their deep unseeing. She did not feel that she was required to give an account of herself in front of the relic but knew that she would have to do so when she was dead, as the others had done. She hoped that judgement would be kind to Lorraine. She hoped that it would be kind to them all.

Following the deaths of Lorraine and Paddy the *Drogheda Independent*'s headline stated that *there are few answers to the double life of Lorraine Farrell,* but which lives? The daily mass-goer with the lace-up latex dress? The popular socialite and the career criminal's girlfriend? The girl who always had a friendly word? The girl who loved her little car, her Peugeot 307? Who went to the races? The girl who took everything into consideration, even writing letters to organize her own funeral rites? We know that she had lost weight in the weeks and months before her death. We know that she was *not herself.* We know that an anonymous friend told the *Sunday World* Lorraine had said *sometimes I let things get in on me.*

This is the border. Beyond the Carlingford bar ships wait on the tide to carry them into the deep channel. When the wind's in the right direction the sound of the heavy marine diesels carries up the lough. There's a tidal bore between Greenore point and the Blockhouse island, a drowning current that'll carry you down and there's a ghost corvette patrolling the boundaries of what's navigable and what will sink you into the unfathomed depths. Sand piles against the railway carriage in Giles Quay, deeper every year and the roof sags and leaks. The carriage windows loosen in their mouldings. The glass shivers in the east wind, salt-whitened panes, blown spindrift in the dunes. The pilot boat chained to its buoy, stern turned seaward in the tidal rush.

Named storms blow up the channel and the Blockhouse island
is lost in spume and spray.

Cowboys Bann had called them and that was the way they
saw themselves, like old-time heroes, grizzled marauders coming
across the border, dust-coated and weary. They ride past
churches knowing that the light is forbidden them, their souls
made forfeit. They will kill and retire into an interior country
and no others will pass that way. Nothing will be forgiven and
no forgiveness will be asked. They will range far beyond the
terrain of themselves, and they will not find their way back.

They had some kind of truth about them. That an enterprise,
even a criminal one, was better than watching your days slip out
from under you. They deserved everything they got, so what
makes the heart weep for men so beholden to their own desire?
Was it that after everything, the theft, the blood, the betrayal,
they believed that they could be redeemed, that the ending
would be something other than they had already ordained for
themselves? They could have told Lorraine. In this place they
kill for politics, they kill for money. Nobody kills for love. In the
end she was the evidence against herself. They all were. Paddy,
Dominic, Brendan and the others. Lorraine had thought there
might have been a world where she could walk with them, be
unwounded, but it was not this one.